The Apothecary of Mantua

For Linda

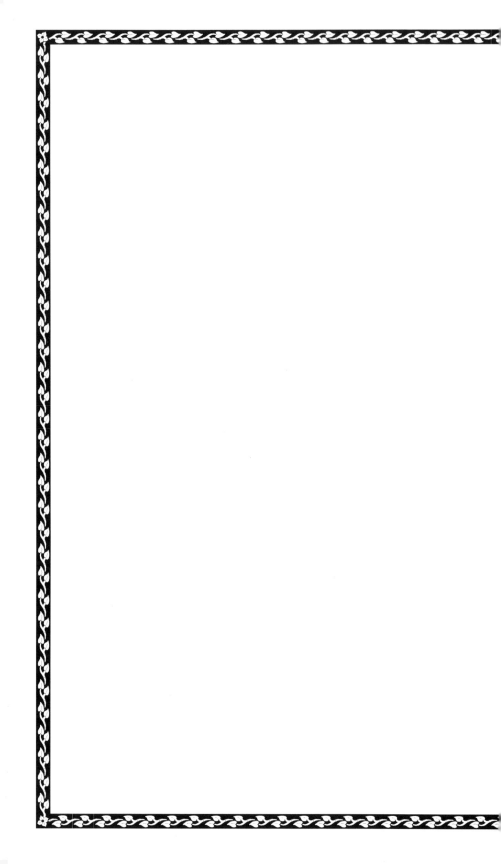

The Apothecary of Mantua

A Supernatural Sequel to Romeo and Juliet

BY

Aaron Hollingsworth

Edited by Katie Thompson

Eightfold Wrath Books

Kansas City

Beta Readers/Critiques: Trish Rasmussen, Phill Layman, Shaada Nettifee, Kevin Phillips, and The Webster Street Critique Group

Images:

Old Man with a Beard by Rembrandt

Rosalind Howard by Dante Gabriel Rossetti

Portrait d'un jeune home by Eustache Le Sueur

A Soldier of the 16th Century by Unknown

Nile crocodile by Hubert Ludwig

Enter Friar Laurence with a Basket by Sir John Gilbert

Juliet by Philip Hermogenes Calderon

All images used are in the public domain.

True, I talk of dreams,
Which are the children of an idle brain,
Begot of nothing but vain fantasy,
Which is as thin of substance as the air...

-Mercutio

<u>Introduction</u>

For centuries, the true moral message of *Shakespeare's Romeo and Juliet* has been debated by scholars and laymen alike. Is it a cautionary tale for teenagers inflicted by the sweet and sudden pangs of love, or was the caution intended for adults who let their conflicts inhibit their duties as parents? Are the authorities of church and state to blame for the tragedy, with so much of the plot dependent on the decisions of Prince Escalus and Friar Lawrence? Perhaps all the characters were to blame despite their best intentions, and so, the lesson is that love and law and faith can do nothing to halt the inevitable conflicts of human beings.

Whilst others ponder these grand theories, I myself have only one question: What did the Apothecary do with the money? Forty ducats back then was the equivalent to $2,000—not a fortune—but enough to change one's station in life if spent wisely. What did this oddly convenient character do after exiting the play? This book is my humble, contrived, convoluted, and black-hearted attempt to answer that question.

This story is told in a bastardized mixture of the Elizabethan style in which The Bard of Avon composed his plays and my own 21st century prose. I hope it is understandable to the layperson while still preserving some of that exquisite 16th century flavor. Also, I admit that I binge-read several Lovecraft stories while writing this, so it might lean that way once in a weird while.

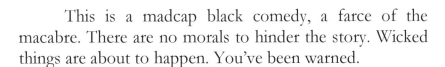

This is a madcap black comedy, a farce of the macabre. There are no morals to hinder the story. Wicked things are about to happen. You've been warned.

Rosaline Capulet – A Lady of the Church

Count Valentine – Brother of Mercutio

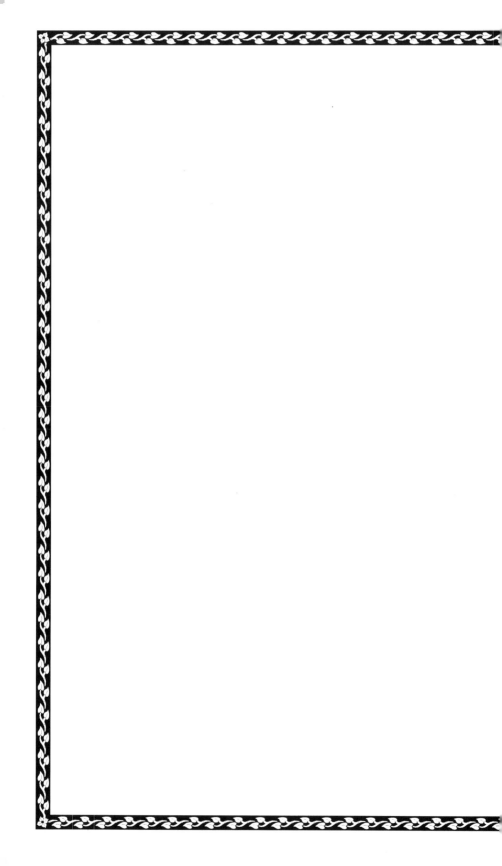

Herald of Papal Army – A Swissman

Henri – A Stuffed Alligator from Egypt

Friar Lawrence – An Alchemist

Juliet Montague – A Ritorno

CHAPTER 1
FORTY DUCATS

The old man hurried to his shop, his thin legs hastened by the power of fresh gold. For the moment, he was rejuvenated by the glee of a handsome profit and the paranoia of his recent crime. But the law had never been his friend—as the youth had told him—neither had the world or Mantua itself. For all his time there, some sixty years, the city had offered him nothing but grief and hardship. Once inside his home and place of business, he shut the door and locked it with a wrought iron key.

Clearing off a space on one of his dusty, splintered tables, he emptied the money pouch to behold and count the shining gold coins. Forty ducats! It was no rich man's fortune, neither was it a meager sum. Still, it was more than he had ever possessed at one time. Using his last three teeth, he bit one of the coins to test it. It was real. They were all real.

"What to do? What to do?" He mumbled as he paced about the shop. "What to do? Aye, but that is not mine only query. Other questions arise in times such as these. Such as how to proceed with what should be done. Or where to go to proceed with these doings, once those doings are determined. Where to proceed is as clear as unstained glass, for I was this morning a hungry citizen and have now become a hungry criminal. 'Twas not greed that compelled me to sell that poison, but poverty. And now with poverty gone, I must proceed with utmost care.

The youth will no doubt use my drug to kill a man or woman who hath earned his hate. Let the crime of murder lie upon his body and soul, for mine both are too thin and brittle."

"Forty ducats! Such a sum can be put to good use no matter how 'twas attained. For criminal or no, I am still an apothecary—a healer of the sick and discoverer of nature's secrets. With this money, I will buy new and exotic herbs with which to make potions. I will invest in rare earthen elements that I will agitate with water and flame, giving birth to new studies of alchemy. I will open a new shop to expand my ambitions and enterprise, but not here. Nay, not in Mantua! My feet I must use to roll the world, so that Mantua will be pressed far from me. To Verona I will go! For it is a city rich with potential patrons, and, yet the better, it is a place whence I can flee to be unknown! Unknown there too shall my crime be, and there shall I use up my days with good food and good deeds. Come, Apothecary! Let my feet work as fast as my drugs! For by tomorrow e'en Verona shall open her arms to our arrival. And there in her heart shall my chambers be!"

The withered druggist, invigorated by ambition, made all the needed preparations for departure. He bought food for the journey, ended up eating it all, and then bought more food. He cleaned his shop the following morning and took from it only three things: a wooden chest containing the tools and goods of his trade, a tortoise shell the size of a small shield, and an eleven-foot stuffed alligator he lovingly called Henri.*[1] After turning in his key to his landlord, he purchased a new robe to replace his old one. It was a fine garment that was modest, yet respectable.

"I must be wary of how much I spend and what I procure," he told himself. "For my load is already burdensome, and this fortune is limited. How now shall we travel, Henri?" he asked his taxidermy pet. "Though thou art light and packed with straw, I shan't carry thee like a fardel on my bent back. We must find a coach that will offer safe and comfortable transport."

---

[1] Henri is actually a crocodile. However, Romeo mistakenly calls him an alligator in the original play. Therefore, for the sake of continuity, we shall refer to Henri as an alligator, even though he's a crocodile.

CHAPTER 2

THE BROKEN FRIAR

He arrived in the city of Verona the following day by coach. He employed the coachman for the entire day to first ensure that he found a stable new residence. While scouring the city for a potential place to dwell and set up shop, the Apothecary spotted a church and bade his driver to stop.

"Wait here," he ordered as he stepped out of the coach. "I must give thanks to the Lord for my recent prosperity." As he approached the massive structure, he whispered low to himself. "I feel it best to give some portion of this money to the church. Five ducats should be a fair trade to cleanse my soul of any wrong I incurred in my dealing with that youth. Yes, four ducats. That should be enough to wrest the burden of my guilt. Three ducats, in the very least."

He walked into the church and found a sad-eyed old man dressed in the humble brown robes of a friar.

"Friar! Oh, how now, good saintly man! Here, take you these three ducats. No! Take you five, no seven! Take you these seven ducats and distribute them to the needs of your followers."

The friar cracked a smile through his morose expression and accepted the money. "Thank you, good sir. 'Twill do the poor well. Though mine eyes be tired and red, I am sure they've never seen you before. Are you newly come to Verona?"

"I am, Friar. I am an apothecary, a healer of the sick and master of the alchemical sciences. I have come to Verona to set up shop."

The friar's eyes brightened briefly. "Alchemy, say you? I, too, practice the art! Or at least, I did until yesternight." His wrinkled eyes brimmed with tears.

"Why, what is the matter, Friar?" the Apothecary asked.

"Nothing, nothing," the friar replied, wiping his tears before they could fall. "It was a terrible lapse in judgment. I must make amends with God for the rest of my life. But, ho, what providence this is, you coming here today of all days. This was no chance meeting, Apothecary. You have come to this city seeking fortune, no doubt. Well, you have found it. In this very church, I keep a laboratory full of the most modern equipment. I have numerous books on the subject and all subjects that relate to the secrets of nature. Take it all, for I have misused it. Take it for your shop and make new discoveries that will benefit your fellow man. Take it with my blessing, good Apothecary."

The two men shook hands, and the Apothecary felt a warm relief wash over him. "Saints be praised!" he thought. "As my fortune dwindles, my fortune grows!"

The friar led the Apothecary down a flight of stone stairs deep below the church. After passing through a long dim hallway, they came to a door that the friar unlocked with an iron key. Once within the laboratory, the Apothecary clasped his hands together in sheer delight. The friar had not exaggerated the magnificence of his equipment.

"Oh, praise God, and thank you, Friar! Prithee, what is thy name?"

"Friar Lawrence," came a woman's voice from behind them.

The two men jumped at the sudden sound. They turned 'round to see a maid appareled in black. She was as beautiful as All Souls Day, yet her eyes were as cold and harsh as Twelfth Night to a heathen.

"Friar Lawrence, I would have words with thee about the sad events of this past week. Two Capulets, two Montagues, and two kinsmen of the prince have departed this world through horrid ends. I wish to uncover the means."

The friar let out a weary sigh. "Good morrow, young Rosaline. I beg that you leave me to my shame. I have already relayed my involvement to the prince, Montague, and thy uncle Capulet. I spent the entirety of yesternight informing them of every secret dealing I had with your poor cousin and her husband."

"Her husband of three days?" Rosaline asked with an edge to her voice. "No, Friar. I have already heard what you told mine uncle. I know that lovelorn fool, Romeo, and my child cousin, Juliet, were divinely join'd by you not two days after I refused the advances of that same impetuous Montague. I saw in him a lack of will that only tempered my resolve to swear off the society of men. And how vexed I was to learn that my brother and cousin both died on Romeo's weapons."

Friar Lawrence furrowed his brow. "Young Lady, Tybalt lived by the sword and so died. And it was Juliet's hand that commanded Romeo's dagger into her breast, not Romeo's! The entire affair was but a tragic, misguided attempt at bringing peace through love. The prince himself deemed it so. Yet, you approach me as if some intended evil had been afoot."

The Apothecary watched the young maid's eyes shift from calm orbs to cruel and discerning spheres, revealing a potent intelligence rarely ever displayed so boldly by a woman. It chilled him to his soul.

Rosaline stepped aggressively toward the friar. "There is more to these sad events than mere tragedy, Friar. The evil you deny is not so easily dismissed by me."

"How dare you, child!" the friar said, lowering his voice. "What authority supports your searing inquisitiveness? You, who have chosen to remain chaste and become a nun, dare to make accusations and demands of me? You must defer to me, girl!"

At this, Rosaline smiled, her face glowing with malicious pride. "A nun? A paramour of Christ? Is that what you heard of me? Oh, poor Friar! How misinformed thou art! No nun am I, nor ever shall I be! While 'tis true I have sworn myself to the church, I belong to a more dire order."

She raised her hand to the friar's eyes, showing him a large ring on her index finger. It was a gold ring with chips of onyx and ruby forming a bold cross. At the very sight of it the friar swiftly lowered his eyes and knelt to the floor.

"How can this be?" he asked in a shocked whisper. "How does a woman of nineteen years gain such a station?"

"By earning it," Rosaline replied. "Now, let it be plain to thee, Friar, that I am not here on behalf of my family. I am the new Inquisitor of Verona. And I say that there *is* an evil machination to these deaths."

The Apothecary froze in fear.

Friar Lawrence trembled and sobbed. "I swear! I swear to you and God and St. Francis above that I meant no ill to the houses of Montague and Capulet! I meant no ill to the prince's kinsmen! I have relinquished every fact there is!"

"Every fact but one!" Rosaline shouted, raising her chin and baring her teeth. "How does a poor friar like you come into possession of a potion that puts the drinker into a death-like sleep, a false death so convincing it robs the breath and beat of heart, but not the life?"

"I created it in this very laboratory, my lady."

"And how came you by the formula?"

9

"I devised and developed it myself, not a fortnight before giving it to your cousin—rest her soul."

The lady inquisitor's eyes narrowed. "What prompted you to invent such a strange elixir? What was its original purpose? It seems strangely convenient for you to have such a substance on hand for such an occasion. Tell me why you made it in the first place!"

The friar shook his head. "I know not! The idea came to me in a dream. It did seem most prophetic at the time. I awoke and all my will was bent on making it. All the knowledge I acquired through years of study melded into a burning inspiration. The dream showed me the way, and I did but follow it! Oh, please forgive me if I have brought shame to our church!"

Rosaline looked up from the tear-filled face of Friar Lawrence. Her cold eyes seemed to reflect some conclusive thought. "So. A dream. Very well, Friar. I thank thee for thy pains and thy help. Good day." She then turned on her heel and left.

Friar Lawrence collapsed into a blubbering stupor. The Apothecary knelt down beside him, placing a hand on his back.

"Good Friar, how came you by this multitude of tears? What calamity hast thou endured?"

The friar wiped his tears and stood up. "I shall tell you it another day, for my tongue and heart are exhausted from the ordeal. Come, good Apothecary. I will help thee locate a place to ply thy trade."

10

CHAPTER 3

THE NOBLE ASSASSINO

The newly appointed count stood solemnly in the crowd of Verona's nobility. By him stood the Prince of Verona, Prince Escalus. Together they watched as the body of their kinsman, Paris, was placed into the family crypt.

"First, my daft brother, Mercutio, and now our soft cousin, Paris," Valentine muttered to the prince. "And both times our family is denied revenge."

"All are punished, Valentine," the prince replied.

Valentine scowled at the words. "Not all, cousin. Not all. Tybalt killed my brother, Mercutio. Romeo killed Tybalt. Then Romeo slew our noble cousin before poisoning himself. Capulet's daughter responded by slaying herself, and then Montague's wife died of grief. But all are not punished."

"Who then, dear cousin, has escaped justice?" the prince asked.

"Did not Romeo's letter to his father state that he bought the poison from an apothecary in Mantua? Is not the sale of such drugs punishable by death there? I would sleep better knowing that this very same apothecary were parted from his mortal coil."

The prince sighed and shook his head. "There must be at least a dozen apothecaries in Mantua. Nonetheless, I will write a letter to Mantua's prince demanding an investigation and just punishment."

Valentine grunted in disapproval. "No, cousin. Let me find the man. 'Twas never my intention to replace Paris as count. This last time let me be what I am: an *assassino*." He laughed bitterly. "If Paris or you had only dispatched me to track down and slay the Montague boy, at least some of this trouble might have been avoided. Paris spent more time signing parchment than on his swordplay. He should not have challenged Romeo. To think, Paris the Count slain by a mere boy…'tis shameful."

The prince sneered. "You care nothing for justice or vengeance, Valentine. You care nothing for this apothecary. You only desire to kill."

Valentine grinned. "I am a man of simple tastes, coz. As an enterprising soldier, I cut many a foreign throat. It mattered not if it was the eve, day, or aftermath of battle. Whilst the blood of other men ran hot with fury only to dry like a summer river, mine own blood ran cold as a spring stream, steady fed by the melting of winter snow. Slaying is a thing to which most men only dream of doing. And dream I did. And dream I still do. Ah, to be the soldier—that fourth age of man—always working toward the advancements of repute and recognition, ever improving. I was not yet ready to move onto this—the fifth age, that of the fatted and fettered justice. But Paris is dead, and I, like a Levite Jew, must wed his burden."

Prince Escalus regarded his kinsman as a maid would regard a newly found blemish. "Do as you will, cousin. Play the soldier *assassino* one last time. But when this apothecary's blood blots out the remainder of thy soul, you will thenceforth abjure thy murderous deeds."

Valentine smiled and bowed in gentlemanly submission. "My Prince is too kind."

"And you are too cruel."

As the doors of the crypt closed upon the bones of Count Paris, the mourners in attendance were startled out of their grief by the sound of Count Valentine's laughter.

CHAPTER 4

VERONA'S HEART

In Verona's heart, the city square, a new sign for all to see was hung. Over a door it swung, emblazoned with a mortar and pestle. Word of the new apothecary reached the ears of the infirm and afflicted. And came they to his shop seeking balm for their ills.

"My knee hurts," said the ghostly bell founder. The old man seemed at first well-preserved in stature and strength. But when he walked, he limped in wincing torment that reddened his pate and stubbly cheeks.

"Have you a seat," bade the Apothecary who put a chair behind him. The bell founder sat and let the Apothecary paw and handle his leg. From a moment's inspection, the Apothecary drew his conclusion as easily as Diane draws her arrow. "Thy knee is old, sir. Older than thee."

"How now?" asked the bell founder.

"A man's body ages more from use than from time. Thy joints are in their twilight years. An honest living brings about honest pains. But worry you not. I have remedy of rejuvenation. Here–" The Apothecary moved on lighted heels to his shelf, from which he drew a jar, from which he drew a powder in heaping spoonfuls into a smaller jar. "Cut from the heads of butchered swine, dried and ground up soft and fine, the ears of pigs be Nature's cure, for the pain you now endure! This powder wilt thou consume once daily with thy midday meal."

"Pig ear?" said the bell founder. "But are those not meant to improve hearing? My other apothecary said as much."

The Apothecary stroked his beard and laughed. "Ha! Where did this fool you speak of learn his healing? England, perchance? Did he learn his trade from a Welsh midwife? Oh, dear man, the pig's ear is composed of the same properties of thy knee's inner joint. Just as a man must consume meat to grow strong, so must you consume this substance to retain thy limb's proper motion. And here, take you this paste and ingest a spoonful. It is butter of the almond mixed with willow tree bark. It will help the pain subside for the present."

The bell founder took the offered dose, stood, and with effort gave a bow. Upon paying for the goods to the Apothecary, he said, "If thy drug's effects match thy words I will sing praises of thee to every laborer I know."

The Apothecary beamed with esteem. "Then ready thy singer's voice anon, good sir, for my drugs are quick. Next customer, please!"

As the bell founder took his leave, a man of middle age approached. Dressed was he in the robes of feigned nobility, bright in colour, but ill of cut. "Good morrow, Apothecary. I am a strumpeteer, an employer of strumpets."

"Ah, a procurer," said the healer with a knowing grin.

"Nay, good sir. For the godly scriptures condemn procurers. Thus, I ply my humble trade by another title."

"As you will, good fellow. How may I service thee?"

"'Tis not I in need of service, but my strumpets. With the summer air heating men's loins, civil strife raising their blood, and recent tragedies marring their hearts, we've been blessed with a torrent of those seeking our custom. My strumpets toil night and day with Verona's sons. I have never been more enriched. And enrichment cries for wise expenditures. I seek contraception for the squishy quims of my fair strumpets, that their bellies remain flat and their obligations constant."

The Apothecary smiled and tittered. "I would be most happy to assist thy strumpets' needs, good strumpeteer. Tell me, how many ladies of the e'en are in thy employ?"

"Two and thirty of the finest loin warmers in all Italia! I should like to buy ten pounds of peacock dung and all the needed herbs to ensure its potency. That should last us the summer, I warrant."

The Apothecary's wrinkled eyes widened in shock. "Peacock dung? By Jove's immaculate beard! I have heard of this foul practice. You intend to make suppositories

17

from this dung to implant in thy strumpets' wombs to make them women of ill carriage."

"Aye, Apothecary. Do I err in this? Must the dung come from a bird of a different feather? I must confess, this is the only means of contraception I've learnt."

The Apothecary raised a finger. "Learnt you nothing 'til this day came. For I tell thee that bird dung of any sort, e'en from the dove that appear'd at Christ's baptism, will not aid thee in the prevention of conception, but 'twill only bring disease and grief to thy strumpets."

The strumpeteer shrank at the old healer's display words. "Very well, sir. Then what must be done?"

The Apothecary formed a ring with his thumb and index finger. "Two and thirty strumpets you have. Two and thirty gold rings wilt thou need, rings of the purest gold to save the strumpets' wombs from unwanted seed."

The strumpeteer frowned and crossed his arms. "Gold rings for my whores? Are you suggesting I marry them off?"

"Nay. I bid thee have these rings fashioned in accord with my design, for no adornments wilt they be, but instruments of sanitary prevention. Up, up, up into the shrill quims they must be placed, held suspend'd by the womb's inner cavity like a halo to hover o'er the heads of thy patron's bulbous members. And when the seed doth flow within the confines of the strumpet's squishy quim, the saintly band will prevent the sin of bastardy. The ring remains affixed within the strumpet evermore until you see fit to retrieve it with an ivory hook to which this purpose must be made."

The strumpeteer shook his head in doubt. "It doth sound costly."

"The sound rings true," said the Apothecary. "'Tis as costly as it is effective and unhazardous. But 'twill be but a single dip in thy purse instead of several dips o'er the years. Furthermore, you can keep the rings as old strumpets are from your employment dismiss'd to be used for new strumpets who come into thy trade."

"And who will insert these rings of heaven's glory?"

"I will perform the deed on the first few strumpets under thine watchful eyes, so as to teach you to do it thyself then and in future days."

When the strumpeteer asked how much it would cost, the Apothecary speedily totaled a sum. An agreement was made, and the Apothecary's heart leapt with delight at the prospect of so handsome a venture. "Two and thirty chalices shalt soon be filled to brim with the seed of man, each one toasting my good fortune! Next customer, please!"

A sullen youth attired in black approached. In his eyes, a deep sorrow. In his hand, a jingling pouch. Leaning in to whisper in the Apothecary's ear, the youth did whisper, "Prithee, apothecary, the matter by which I call is dire and must be shrouded in discretion. Here come I with money in hand to purchase silence as well as remedy."

The Apothecary nodded and rubbed his hands together. "Aye, good young sir. 'Tis shrewdness I then prescribe." Waving about his spindly arms, he addressed the other patrons in the shop. "Hence, hence! Prithee, hence! This young lord must needs my observance. When he departs without, you may all return to buy my cures."

When the patrons departed and both were alone, the Apothecary sat the youth down at a small table. "Now, my lord, tell me thy hurts."

"'Tis not my hurts for which I come, but mine uncle's, though we share the same hurt. A dark cloud has descend'd upon our house. In these last days few, my noble uncle Montague hath lost a wife, a son, and a daughter-in-law."

"Dear me. Were they by plague taken, or some other malady, or need you me to identify the sickness lest it spreads?"

"The sickness hath already run its course throughout our house, for it is of grief I speak. Grief did slay mine uncle's wife, son, and daughter-in-law. The wife died agriev'd at the death of their son, who had poison'd himself at the death of his new wife, though true death it weren't. And the daughter-in-law slew herself with her husband's dagger upon seeing he did poison himself for her."

20

The Apothecary grasped his beard in sympathy. "Oh, what terrible transpirations! Tell me, how did these sad events unfold?"

The youth shook his head and sighed. "'Tis a sad story I had relay'd already too much these past days few. Ask around this dismal city, and thou wilt learn the tragedy. I come not as a page, good man, but a customer."

"Of course, my lord. What help dost thou seek?"

"Mine uncle doth presently drown his sorrow in drink. Our house doth grow dryer with his every fit of grief, which are many and frequent. But it doth not help, and I fear our prized collection of wines will soon be wasted on present melancholy rather than invested in future cheers. Have you not some drug that brings about a drunken calm? For it is dull serenity mine uncle endeavors to find."

"Such drugs I have," the Apothecary said with a slow nod. "But it is death to anyone who over-uses them. I import them from the deepest wilds of Ethiopia, the ports of Turkey, and the far-off onshores of Cathay. These heathen cures can surely become heathen curses if not used in moderation. I will assemble a special mixture of these drugs with thine uncle's sorrow in mind but will sell you only so much per week, lest he desire too much drug too soon."

The youth smiled, though still sadly, and placed the jingling pouch upon the small table. "Here is for the first of the doses. When shall I return for them?"

"I shall have them ready on the morrow. What name shall I write on the parcel, my lord?"

The youth rose up and gave a courteous bow. "Benvolio of House Montague."

CHAPTER 5

A LATISH DISCOVERY

He closed the book between his spotty hands and held it to his lips in thought. Curiosity, Possibility, and Implication conjoined into a braid—a rope in the Apothecary's mind. Where that rope led and to what end, he knew not. The hour was late, yet the night of study had distracted him from his weariness. The laboratory table at which he sat stirred with flickering flames, bubbling fluids, shining glass, and slow-dripping taps. Ensconced candles lit a plethora of paraphernalia hanging from wall and rafter: maps, charts of strange geometry, eldritch instruments, a tortoise shell, and Henri the stuffed alligator. With eyes lit by embers of curiosity, the Apothecary stroked his tattered beard whilst looking the dead beast in its glass eyes. Henri stared back, an eleven foot long monster dangling still and silent on strings of wire.

"A formula that simulates death. To what purpose would such a potion serve?" the Apothecary asked the preserved pet. "The friar did inform his mistress that this formula came to him in a dream. Truly Henri, 'tis a brilliant design of medicine. But why? Why invent a dram that creates the signs of decease? To, perchance, impose a deep sleep to aid recovery of an already present ill or injury? Nay, this formula contains too much sumac. 'Twould hinder the body's regenerative powers."

He opened the book to glance at the formula again. "'Tis far too ingenious to neglect, yet lends itself naught to practicality." He looked back at the alligator and smiled, his nigh toothless grimace in contrast to a grin of countless fangs. "Would that either of us had the answer, old friend. All the same, thou art a charitable listener to my fruitless ramblings." He raised his frail hand and passed it fondly over Henri's snout.

With a weary sigh, he returned to his reading. As the hour passed, his cares grew light as his eyelids grew heavy. Slowly slumping in his chair, the Apothecary fell into a gentle slumber.

Not far away, a tiny queen's carriage, almost too small to be seen, made its way underneath the narrow space below the laboratory door and across the floor of the room's confines. The carriage was the hollow shell of a hazelnut covered with grasshopper wings, traced with spider webs, and collared with eerie blue light. It was pulled by a team of tiny, scurrying insects yet unnamed by man. The waggoneer, a small grey-coated gnat, whipped vigorously at them with a lash of spider film. Wheels with spider leg spokes spun like four pennies rolling on the floor, carrying the nut, its driver, and its mysterious passenger onward to the venerable form sleeping in the towering chair.

"Is the Apothecary in sight, Benito?" came a woman's voice from within the nut.

"Aye, Your Grace," answered the gnat, a boisterous cruelty in his segmented features. "Yon he slumbers in his chair, his ear too aloof for climbing. I must ask Her Magnificence to sit fast."

"Do as thou must," the woman's voice replied.

The gnat's claw-like mouth chittered and buzzed a strange command, and great wings unfolded from the atomies' bodies. With a crack of the gnat's whip, the scurrying team became a droning chorus of regimented pullers. Up, up, up the carriage went, through the stale air of the musty laboratory and into the large and veiny ear of the Apothecary. The old man shuddered in his sleep as the team of flying vermin pulled the nut and its occupant deeper into his ear canal, past his ear drum, and into the very brain of he who slept. And as he slept, he did dream a dream not of his own making.

After fourteen minutes, the bugs, the gnat, the nut and its occupant emerged from the Apothecary's opposite ear, flying down to the floor, and escaping back beneath the locked wooden door.

The Apothecary woke with a start, his bleary eyes searching aimlessly, his frail arms trembling. He grasped the book on the table and read the formula in a mad, mumbling whisper.

Added in this order to this potion make,

A sleep like death from which to wake,

Nightshade pick'd on a tempest night,

Foxglove pick'd when the moon shown bright,

Deadman's Bells clipp'd on stony bluff,

Quartz powder ground from uncut rough,

Saint John's Wort and eglantine,

Boil'd to broth in unbless'd wine,

Cyprus root dug with iron spade,

Near a yard where a lich was laid,

Stew these parts in a cauldron of copper,

And store in a vial with a tight lead stopper.

He set the book down and stood, his mind a racing mechanism of inspiration. To and fro, back and forth, he paced in giddy frenzy.

"Why Henri, 'tis simple, a matter of substantial reversal, applying laws of alchemy both secret and universal! To prepare the formula through inverse means. Combining components in retreating scheme, I can undo the effects that death doth render; bestill'd hearts to action and stiff joints to tender. Breath that sucks in and outwardly expel; ears that once more hear the chime of bell; eyes that doth see and mouths that doth speak, merry! A drug that returns life's color to cheeks. The good friar's drug was a false-death potion, but this new formula wilt to the dead give motion. 'Twill not simulate death but counterfeit life, or perhaps bring back those sever'd by the Reaper's scythe!"

With jubilant glee, the Apothecary locked eyes with his suspended pet. "My dear friend and assistant, we've

26

work to do! By Mercury's vessel, a new discovery shall be made, a new idea birth'd!"

CHAPTER 6

THE COMELY INQUISITOR

In a private study filled with books and scrolls and charts of strange geometry, the Inquisitor of Verona sat at her desk reading a letter. Before her were two lictors—tall, sturdy men armed with foils.

"Dreams," Rosaline said, resting her pale chin upon her crossed fingers. "Some would say they are the spawn of an idle brain. If so, who plants the seed in such a fertile place as a man's mind?" She looked to one of her lictors. "Michelangelo, did not God speak prophecies through the dreams of Joseph of Israel?"

"E'en so, Inquisitor."

"And, did not Joseph the husband of Mary receive dreams from God's messengers to take the woman as wife and to escape to Egypt?"

"E'en so, Inquisitor," the lictor replied stoutly.

"And, if the Holy Father sees fit to guide us through dreams, then would not the Devil and his minions do the same?"

At this, the lictor had no words with which to answer, for indeed, he was wary to do so.

Rosaline smiled and stood. "God gave such power to the angels, and Lucifer was the first. It stands to reason that the Enemy could at least copy the craft, yes?"

The two lictors regarded one another, confusion betraying stern expressions.

Rosaline scoffed and threw up her hands. "Perhaps a man's mind is not as fertile as I thought!"

The door to the study opened, and in walked a third lictor, who knelt in greeting and obedience.

"Rise Guiducci," Rosaline commanded. "What news bring you from Mantua?"

The lictor answered as he rose. "Six apothecaries in as many days, Inquisitor. The city of Mantua is now without healers."

"Did you discover and dispatch the murderer?"

"Nay, but discover'd I the pattern of his art. He did use a heat'd stiletto, the blade hot enough to fuse flesh. Each wound was to the heart, and not a drop of blood spill'd." A flash of anger lit the lictor's dark eyes. "Would that I had caught the assassino in the act. Three apothecaries would still be alive."

Rosaline waved in dismissal. "You tried in that regard. Have you any summation as to why these murders—nay, assassinations—were carried out?"

"Nay, Inquisitor. Though the method be a sound one, the cause seems madness."

"In one form or another," Rosaline agreed with a nod. "Thou art certain the assassinations stopp'd with the apothecaries?"

"Aye, Inquisitor. I remain'd three days after the last apothecary's slaying, and no such killing occur'd thence."

Rosaline pursed her lips and paced about the room, her lictors moving from her path. "These deaths are of a cunning evil, someone who delights in the destruction of healers. Should he know it or not, this assassino is the Devil's servant."

Guiducci glanced at his fellows. "Shall we resume the inquisition on this matter, my lady?"

"Nay," said Rosaline as she covered her hair with a black shawl. "Worse things are afoot here in Verona. The plights of other cities we can but note and tend to as we can. Come, you all. We must inquist the dreamers of this city, those weak of will and sensitive of mind."

"To what end?" asked Michelangelo.

The Inquisitor smiled, her face beautifully terrifying. "Not *what* end, good man, but whose."

CHAPTER 7

A PLEA OF HUNGER

The desired knock came at the desired hour. The Apothecary, clumsy in his giddiness, nearly fell as he stumbled to his shop door. Pulling the portal open, his old eyes swelled as he took in the sight of his visitor.

"Friar Lawrence, you came! Praise God and be welcome, dear benefactor."

The friar entered and doffed his rough spun cloak. Though his face smiled and showed true politesse, he did look a whole ten years older from their last meeting. "Benedicite, good Apothecary. I pray my old equipment hath brought thee thy fortune sought."

"It hath, and more so," the Apothecary said, grinning. "Come ye down to the laboratory. A new discovery I've made, by aid of one of thy own alchemical devices. Since thou art the source of mine invention, 'tis my wish to demonstrate my finding to you first of all men."

The somber friar's weary eyes lit with good humor. "It cheers me to see a fellow alchemist so alighted with newfound knowledge, be it by my make or no. Lead on, good man. Show me thy mixer's miracle."

Down a winding spiral of stairs they went, through the bolted door, into the alchemist's den, where table stood and alligator hung therein.

"Whence did you get such a magnificent specimen?" asked the friar as he marveled at the suspended beast.

"Ah, Henri," the Apothecary said, patting the stuffed animal's head. "I acquired him from a French sailor who sold me a crate of mandrake root. How he acquired such a great curiosity, I know not. He told me only that the lizard was Egyptian in origin and might've belonged to a great pharaoh. I considered giving him an Egyptian name, but seeing as how the Frenchman made it to me a gift of sorts, a French name seem'd more fitting. So, Henri he did become, a kingly name for a kingly beast."

The friar arched a bushy eyebrow and crossed his arms. "Methinks lions are more kingly than alligators."

The Apothecary shrugged. "On land, 'tis true. But in rivers deep the alligator is unrival'd; for he hath an adder's stealth, a lion's bite, and more patience than a dame with spite. But come, come. To the table turn thy studious gaze and witness what was impossible but three days ago."

Three jars, all alike in size and shape, and a vial of dark liquid on the table stood. The jars were empty save a single dead spider residing in each bottom. The first spider was shriveled and dry, its legs curled inward. The second was impaled on a small pin and likewise curled.

The third was smashed and contorted, as though stomped by a grinding heel.

In a scholarly voice, the Apothecary began his presentation. "Here hath we three arachnids, all of a kind and age. The first, starved. The second, stabbed. The third, crushed. Yet, tho' death hast conquer'd, he hath not claim'd. Observe ye, good friar."

With deft care and steady hand, the Apothecary took up the vial of black liquid, removed the stopper, and let drip a single drop onto each spider's corpse.

Friar Lawrence watched and waited, his present cares and woes forgotten as his rational brain tingled with the potential for wonder.

The spiders stirred. The starved arachnid flipped from its back to spread its legs and scurried about in frantic search of escape. The impaled spider did likewise spring about though hindered much by the pin through its middle. The squished spider did not move from its spot, even though its few intact legs did flicker with haunting efficiency.

Friar Lawrence trembled, half in fear, half impressed. "Are they alive?" he asked in a shuddering whisper.

The Apothecary shook his head. "Nay. 'Tis only the appearance of life. At present, a mere trick of elements and nerves. With more research and experimentation, perhaps a true cure for death can be render'd from this formulistic device."

"How came you to make this formula?"

"'Tis derived from one of thine, good friar. Your potion that, once imbib'd, brings about the appearance of death. I did but reverse the order in which the ingredients were combined. Here, in these jars, you see the result."

At first, the friar smiled, a glint of flattered pride twinkling in his eyes. Then his features grew long and shook with deep sadness. Grief erupted from his eyes in the form of tears and his mouth in the form of sobs.

"My good friend, what is the matter?" the Apothecary asked, placing a hand on the friar's shoulder. "I've not known you a fortnight, yet I can see that this is not thine usual humor. Prithee, tell what is the source of thy grief? Did you not make mention of it at our first meeting and swear to tell me all? I may be a mere healer of the body and not of the spirit. Yet, I dare suggest that confession, be it to a man of the cloth or a simple man as me, is good for the soul."

The friar sat down in a nearby chair. "'Tis a tale I've had to repeat a hundred times this fortnight last. Telling it again will to me no succor give. But if you are to hear it, it is best to come from the horse's mouth, as they say. The formula thou didst derive thy elixir from, I made use of it on a young woman, but it only led her to death."

The Apothecary frowned. "It dispatched her with real death instead of false?"

"Nay, the potion worked well, too well, sir. No poisoning but a perfect death-like sleep it did render."

The friar sniffled and wiped his wet eyes. "To the beginning I must go, for the story is as tangled as it is sad."

"Romeo, a son of House Montague, was husband to Juliet, only daughter of House Capulet. Their love bloom'd despite warring households, and how that war started, no man can say. I married them, at first in secret but with the hope that the union would bring the feud to peace. Alas, Tybalt, cousin to Juliet, slew Mercutio, Romeo's foremost friend. And Romeo did slay Tybalt in turn."

"Banished, Romeo fled from the city, his marriage to Juliet still unknown. Juliet was a pining wretch; not for her cousin did she mourn, but for the absence of her new husband. Her parents would have married her perforce to County Paris. Then came she to me, and with wild looks bid me devise some means to rid her from this second marriage, or in my cell there would she kill herself. Then gave I her, so tutored by my art, that same sleeping potion, which so took effect as I intended, for it wrought on her the form of death."

"In the meantime, I wrote to Romeo, that he should hither come as this dire night to help to take her from her borrowed grave, being the time the potion's force should cease. But he which bore my letter, Friar John, was stayed by accident and returned my letter back. Then, all alone, at the prefixèd hour of Juliet's waking, came I to take her from her kindred's vault, meaning to keep her closely at my cell till I conveniently could send to Romeo."

"But when I came, some minute ere the time of her awakening, there in the church untimely lay the noble Paris and true Romeo dead. Paris was slain by Romeo's sword. Romeo, by poison coiffed in suicide. Juliet awoke, and I entreated her come forth, and bear this work of heaven with patience. But then a noise did scare me from the tomb. And she, too desperate, would not go with me, but, as it seems, did violence on herself by stabbing her own heart with Romeo's dagger."[2]

The friar paused to bow his head. "All was discover'd, that grisly scene of death, by the prince, Montague and Capulet all. I confess'd my entire involvement, and the prince, in a godly show of mercy did spare my life. United in grief, Montague and Capulet took hands and ended their years-long feud. All are punished. Montague lost a son. Capulet, a daughter. And I, oh I! I have lost son and daughter both, for I did wed them and raise them on the heavenly word since they were children."

The friar trembled and wept. "And, but children they were, good Apothecary! Romeo, no more than seventeen. And sweet Juliet, on the verge of fourteen!"

The still open black vial filled with its miraculous potion trembled in the Apothecary's hand. He recalled the youth who had bought his poison in Mantua, the youth whose face was as fair as it was grim, the youth who paid him the forty ducats that changed the man's life. In his heart, he felt a hot spike invade. It was regret. He wanted to stay quiet. He wanted no part of this tragedy, but the

---

[2] As the good friar has no doubt repeated this sad tale to numerous persons by this point, the author saw fit to simply utilize the original text from the play in which he summarizes the events of the tragedy.

words came out, and he hadn't the will or wisdom to stop them.

"I... I... Prithee, Friar, how..." he swallowed through a dry throat. "How didst this Romeo come by the poison?"

The friar adjusted himself in the chair and sighed. "Mantua, where he was refuged. I recall now that he had sent a letter to his father explaining his actions and impending suicide. He procured the poison from an apothecary there."

The two old men regarded one another with a shock of realization, as though they beheld the faces of ghosts and not men. Their hearts did quake and limbs did shake. Friar Lawrence stood as if a hangman's rope had pulled him to his feet. "You?" the friar shouted.

The Apothecary cringed and bowed his head. "Oh spiteful fate! Oh un-cleansable sin! I tried to flee and hide hence inside a lion's den!"

With a rigid finger, the friar poked the Apothecary's sunken chest. "You sold dear Romeo that poison? You ruined my perfect plan to unite two households in love instead of untimely death?"

Shivering and nodding with wretched sobs, the Apothecary answered. "Aye, aye. I sold it to him."

"For how much, thou devil! Thirty pieces of silver?"

"'Twas forty ducats, more money that I've e'er had. But I vowed to use it for good, to thenceforth heal and help my fellow man."

"Holy Saint Francis!" the friar cried with a stamp of his foot. "The Prince of Verona must hear of this. Stay you here, thou devilish peddler, and pray for the Lord's mercy on thy rotted soul!"

The friar turned toward the door.

The Apothecary reached to halt him. "Nay, Friar, wait!"

"Take off thy hands!"

The friar shoved the frail old man back. Stumbling, the Apothecary fell against the hanging alligator and unknowingly spilled the black potion atop the dead beast's head. The friar was nearly out the laboratory door when the Apothecary sprang forth and dived at the holy man's legs.

"Mercy!" the Apothecary cried, wrapping his spindly arms about the friar's ankle. "I was hungry! Hungry! My plea is not one of guilt nor innocence, but hunger! My poverty did concede to the bargain, not my will! I was hungry!"

"Unhand me, poisonous devil! The burden of my guilt shall be pass'd o'er to thy stoop'd shoulders once the prince has you rightfully punish'd. Hinder not a man of God!"

"Blame not a desperate man!" the Apothecary mewled, squeezing the leg all the tighter.

The two old men struggled with no avail to either side. With all his might, the Apothecary squeezed 'til his wrinkled eyes shut from the strain. He heard a heavy thud on the floor, and the friar screamed. The holy man's leg broke out from his meager hold.

"No!" the Apothecary cried, opening his eyes and reaching out the door.

But the friar was not without. The Apothecary heard the man's muffled screams right behind him. He

40

rolled over and beheld the friar, his shouting head and most of his shoulders trapped inside the alligator's spread jaws. The long, sinuous bulk that was Henri was now off his wires, splayed on the floor like a giant dog, worrying the kicking form of the trapped friar. Through cloth, flesh, and bone the beast's fangs tore. The Apothecary froze in horror as Henri whipped and shook Friar Lawrence like a caught cat. Bone crunched, and the ghostly friar gave up the ghost. The beast's jaws opened again to envelope the man's entire corpse, the muscles in its gullet ushering the dead to the dark crypt that was the alligator's belly.

From aforth the shriveled loins of the shaking Apothecary, a pint of piss flooded his robes.

Henri looked at him through glass eyes now lit with unnerving awareness. "Close the door," the monster said, its voice a hollow, hissing rumble. "Lessst we be dissscover'd."

Crawling and scooting, the Apothecary obeyed and used his back to push shut the laboratory door. For the next moment, he sat there, regarding his unstrung pet and contemplating death.

"Henri, why? Why did you eat the friar?"

The alligator's mouth was a long trap of teeth, devoid of lips to render expression. Yet, the old man thought he spied a smile.

"I was hungry," Henri said.

CHAPTER 8

THE DISGRACED NURSE

Alone, and yet surrounded, the old woman addressed any and all that passed by. Her face, hands, and garments were many days unwashed, stained with the filth of the street and reeking of her sweat. Haggard and disheveled, she spread her hands, stooped, and repeated her offer again and again in the busy street.

"Lords and ladies, has anyone need for a nurse? Do you have little pretty ones in need of tending? I ask no wages, my lords and ladies, only refuge from these horrible streets. Oh, please, will you not hear me? Am I already a ghost, curs'd to walk unseen and unheard?"

"What qualifications have you?" a man asked.

The woman's eyes sparked with hope. There was also a bit of madness there.

"I will withhold no secrets, milord, for doing so hath brought me ruin. For three and twenty years, I was nurse to the babes of House Capulet. Nary a complaint had their parents about my conduct. But, alas, all of that generation's lost to God, in some way. The earth did swallow all my former master's hopes. The first three died all of sickness, nothing to be done. Poor Tybalt died as he liv'd, by the sword. Rosaline did commend herself to th' church—a saintly maid. And poor Juliet, oh the prettiest babe e'er I nursed, did die a victim of young love's unmerciful lure!"

"Enough, woman!" the man interrupted with a raised hand. "I and Verona all have heard that tragic tale by now. I ask only this, were you dismissed by Lord Capulet or didst thou leave of thy own accord?"

"I was rudely and harshly dismiss'd, milord," the nurse growled, her few teeth bared in anger. "Capulet cast me to the lonely and dirty streets without a penny to feed myself. He would have struck me dead with his long sword if not for his Lady wife's merciful heart. Betrayer they called me! Procurer and sluttish matchmaker, they said, and worse!"

The man chuckled. "Aye, me. This angle of the story wilt go good around my dinner table tonight. Go on, continue, wretched woman. Make me laugh again, and I will surely give thee a penny."

The nurse's eyes swelled in outrage. "Off with you, lack-chinned wastrel! Thou milkless, shaggy brute of a man! I would not raise your children if Jove commanded it! Off with you!"

The man laughed again and tossed a penny at her. The tiny coin bounced off her chest and fell to the dusty stone ground. As the man walked off, the nurse began to start after him but changed her mind. To her knees she went, sobbing and looking for the small copper disk. "Oh, lamentable life," she sighed between sobs. With eyes blurred from age and tears, the nurse searched in vain. "Lost," she sighed. "Lost… all lost…"

There was a jingle beneath her, and beheld she not a coin of copper, but of silver. "A shilling?" she gasped, grabbing up the small treasure. She looked up to see who had tossed it, and her red eyes lit with joy.

"Rosaline! The prettiest babe e'er I nursed! Oh, heavens bless thee!"

The Inquisitor of Verona gazed down at the destitute woman. At Rosaline's flank were her three lictors. "God g'ye good morrow, sweet nurse. I have need of thee. If that need doth prove useful, I will to thee employment give."

The nurse stood, her beady eyes narrowing.

"Thy tone is odd, young lady. To what purpose do you charge me? Who are these men? They have a sinister look to them."

The Inquisitor's eyes shifted left and right. "This street is too crowded, too many eyes and ears." She turned and walked away, her black cloak lapping after her.

The nurse felt the lictors' hands take hold, and they ushered her forth to follow their mistress. When she tried to speak, the grips tightened. The lictors held her arms, and she, her tongue.

They came to a tavern full of hungry patrons. Rosaline called for a table in a private parlor. The timid nurse was made to sit betwixt two lictors. Rosaline and the third sat across the table. "A side of mutton, rigatoni prima vera, and red wine for all," ordered the lady in black.

"Aye, my lady. How will you be paying?" asked the host, a short, balding man with a practiced smile.

Rosaline cast her piercing stare at the nurse. "Pay the man. We are all hungry."

The silver coin was still in the nurse's hand. The old woman glanced down at it as though it were her newborn child.

"But, dear Rosaline, you only just gave me this. 'Twill cost the whole coin to feed us all."

The Inquisitor said nothing. She merely maintained her nigh-tangible beam of attention on the wretched nurse.

The nurse shrank and thought, "Did I truly raise this cold-hearted creature?" She glanced around the table at the tall and broad lictors. All stared back eerily out of the corners of their eyes. She looked to the host who stood by the table, waiting. A part of her died as she handed the man the coin.

The wine and food was served. When the parlor was clear of staff, Rosaline and her lictors bowed their heads. The nurse meekly followed suit.

Rosaline spoke. "Blessed be this bounty, for it is the flesh of the Lamb. Blessed be this wine, for it is the blood of the Lamb. The body of Christ is our only sustenance. Amen."

46

"Amen," repeated the lictors.

"A-Amen," stammered the nurse.

All began to eat and drink, but that did not keep the nurse silent. "Here now, Rosaline, what be the meaning of this?" she asked between bites of sheep's flesh and bread. "Why treat me with such cruelty, giving me money only to force expense upon me? I was liken to thy mother, had the poor lady survived thy birth."

Rosaline washed rigatoni down with wine. Sternly, she did say, "You, like my mother? Never."

"But I raised you in her place—you and Tybalt both. 'Twas thy dying mother who bid me do the task."

Rosaline shook her head. "The only mother I've known is the Blessed Virgin Mary. The woman that birth'd me went to heaven with a different role to play. And you, your role as nurse is ended. No one wants the nurse who led a young girl to her doom."

The old woman slapped the table. "Juliet drank that potion! Juliet took up the boy's dagger and did stab that heart I lov'd! Not I! Not I!"

Rosaline drained her cup and then held it out for a lictor to fill again. "It was you who help'd orchestrate her marriage to Romeo, yes? She had thy full support in the union, though her hand was not thine to give."

The Inquisitor's eyes hardened, and her face became a porcelain mask of discernment.

"You spoil'd that girl. You did not wean her til she reached the age of six. You did pilfer cakes for her between meals. You gave her more attention than any of us. And when womanhood she reach'd, you allowed her to indulge in pleasures of a man's flesh."

"They were married, Rosaline."

The Inquisitor tilted her head. "Yes. They were. And, knowing this, you tried to convince her to marry County Paris whilst still married to Romeo. Such ill advice would have made her an adulteress twice over."

The old woman slowly put down her fork. "How didst thou know I advised her so?"

Rosaline sighed, as if in relief. "And now we've arrived at the matter I wish to address. As I said, you always indulged poor Juliet, never told her nay. To her you gave all and with her agreed all…until you saw fit to advise her to abandon her husband for a man you knew she would not and could not love. Why?"

The old woman trembled, her eyes betraying apprehension. "The only one I told this to was—."

"—Friar John," Rosaline interrupted. "He told me of your confession to him in a letter."

"Then you know he did absolve me!"

Rosaline shook her head. "This is not about the tidiness of your simple soul, woman. You told Friar John of a dream you had, a dream that compell'd you to advise Juliet to marry Paris. Tell me of this dream, and how it did

48

prompt you to, at last, go against Juliet's wants and wishes."

The old woman glanced about uncomfortably at her present company. All her waking existence, she had ever done as she was told. Now could be no exception.

"I'd just arrived from my meeting with Romeo. I was sore and winded from walking. I told Juliet that the Montague youth awaited her in Friar Lawrence's cell, there to exchange vows and be married. She left at once, and I, tired from playing the messenger, went to bed and slept the noon hence."

"Oh, what a dream it was! Nightmarish, at first, but it ended well, aye. I dreamt that Romeo did transmogrify into a headless serpent's body. Though it struck and struck the poor maid, the foul thing could not inject its venom into her, for it had no fangs with which to pierce. Paris then took her up in his arms and carried her into a grand new house."

"When I awoke I learnt that Tybalt slew that crude oaf, Mercutio, and Romeo slew Tybalt in turn. Romeo was banished, and poor Juliet was, by the law's charge, separat'd from her new husband. I, too, learn'd the County Paris sought her hand, and so, thinking on the dream, I did advise her to marry the good suitor, who did already love her true enough as that Romeo did. That was why I advised her so. The dream did seem to portend to some avenue of salvation." She began to weep. "But it did only incite her rebellion. Oh, how evil I must have seemed to her, to drive her to such desperations!"

"Thought you the dream unusual?" Rosaline asked.

The old woman restrained her blubbering. "Aye, for I rarely dream at all."

The Inquisitor sat back and rested her head on a lictor's shoulder, her eyes blank in thought. "I would say that you, too, were ill advised."

"By whom?"

The Inquisitor sat up and faced forward. "By whomever gave you that dream. Tell me, you were a midwife once; have you heard of Queen Mab, the fairies' midwife?"

Puzzled, the old woman shook her head.

Rosaline shrugged. "Oh well. Our business is then concluded, sweet nurse. I and my lictors must away. Help thyself to the remainder of our meal. There is still plenty."

As the Inquisitor and her men rose from the table, the old woman stood, her hands clasped in supplication.

"Oh, leave me not to a life of poverty, dear Rosaline!"

The Inquisitor paused. "What is so bad about a life of poverty? When sworn to such, it can be most rewarding. Get you to the church. Seek Friar John again. To ensure your salvation of soul and body, you must take a vow of poverty *and* silence. Do this, and submit yourself to the holy house of God, and you will never go hungry or sleep in the street again. I will only give you this offer once. Now, get you gone. I've an evil to catch."

CHAPTER 9

THE PRINCE'S LEAVE

"Six men, Valentine! Six apothecaries slain by thee!" the prince admonished, striking his cousin about the face.

Grim and stoic, the assassino's head did not even turn from the blow.

The two nobles glared at one another in the prince's lavish council room with a ceiling high as the prince's authority. They were alone.

"Better it were seven," said Valentine.

The Prince of Verona struck him again with a closed fist. This time, the Count's head turned, and his lip split to weep blood. Still, his expression was unchanged.

Enraged, the Prince of Verona paced about the marble-floored room, stepping hard as he did so. "Murderer," he muttered. "Were it not for our kinship, I would see thee hanged."

Valentine grinned. "Nay, coz. You've not the courage to order a man's death. Why, you can merely slap my face as though it were Lord Capulet's wrist."

The words bit the prince deeply. "Make not a jest of the mercy I showed Lord Capulet or Montague, for it is the same mercy I am showing thee now."

Valentine laughed. "You show naught but a front, cousin. But a pleasing and comely front it is, one worthy of a prince." The Count's grin melted. "But forget not who kept you in power. Forget not that Valentine, not you, maintained our sovereignty by secretly pitting Montague against Capulet these five years gone. Both houses were growing in strength, each a threat to our own. Were it not for my assassinations and rumor-mongering, their feud would never have begun, and we might have been ousted had they join'd arms against us."

The prince shook his head and waved as though refusing an unsavory dish. "The feud went on for too long. Too much blood was spilt. I am sick of blood, Valentine. I pray that you now are, in the very least, sated by it."

Valentine shrugged. "Sated I would be, had not the truly guilty apothecary fled my vengeance. Did I not say, 'Better it were seven'?"

Now, the Count began to pace about, though his footfalls made little sound. "I did not simply run through every apothecary I encounter'd in Mantua. I approach'd them all in friendly fashion, at times as a patron seeking custom, other times as a stranger in a dark street. I would engage them into ample talk by throwing or showing gold, for most were poor and without friends. I found in these talks that there were seven apothecaries in Mantua. And, to the sad fate of six and a former landlord, I learned that the oldest and poorest and most pitiable apothecary in that town had recently vacat'd and relocat'd to Verona."

With wide eyes, the Count grinned like the Devil. "He is here, coz. By repute of Mantua, the poorest apothecary did come to our city with twenty to fifty ducats to his name. Did not old Montague receive a letter stating that Romeo did pay a poor apothecary forty ducats for that poison?"

Flustered, the prince rubbed his brow. "Valentine, I have ever trusted your skill of deduction. Your talent for finding truths is second'd only by your talent for slaying men. You've a rogue's heart but a keen mind. And though you walk a dark road, your sins have always serv'd the greater needs of our house. Art thou sure this is the same apothecary who broke the law of selling mortal drugs?"

Valentine nodded gravely. "It can be no other, coz. Let me put my burning blade in his heart, and there I shall leave the dagger to rust, never to kill again. Let the assassino do his work, and thou wilt have assassinat'd the assassino. A goodly count I will ever be, that will only draw his sword in defense of the innocent."

The prince sighed and sat down at the grand table that took up a portion of the great room. "All the death that we've wrought, it can finally end tonight?"

"It can and will, by thy leave."

The prince clasped his hands, partly in prayer, partly to rest his head upon them. "I bid thee go then. You have my leave. Be sure to steal some objects of value and money. Make it look like a robbery, yourself, the robber. Get thee hence."

Wordless and eager, Count Valentine took his leave of the weary and guilt-laden Prince of Verona.

CHAPTER 10

THE BURNING BLADE

The hour was late in the Apothecary's shop, yet cared he not. His every sense was alerted by and focused on the youth before his counter, Benvolio of Montague. The parcel of drugs meant for the youth's uncle lay on the counter between them as the sullen youth recounted his version of the recent tragedy.

"And now," Benvolio said with a sigh. "I will never again see Romeo's smile, nor his frown, for both were becoming on his tender face. I will never again hear clever Mercutio's jests and jibes. He and Romeo enhanc'd each other, inspir'd one another since childhood. They were best of friends, and I did bask in the light of their friendship."

Leaning on the wooden counter, the Apothecary regarded the youth with teary eyes and wet cheeks.

"I am so, so sorry," he said with a controlled whimper.

Benvolio smiled sadly and gave a weak shrug. "I have shed my tears for them, though they will always be miss'd. Their suffering ended with their deaths." He looked down at the parcel of drugs. "Would that mine uncle's suffering would also end."

The Apothecary wiped his eyes with the sleeve of his robe. "Are my drugs not working for him?"

"They work as well as strong wine. Yet, I fear there be no cure for the loss of a son and wife on the same day."

The Apothecary stroked his beard in thought. "I will see what else can be done. You've my word on that, my lord."

Benvolio gave a bow and took up the parcel. "I must bid thee good night."

The Apothecary returned the bow with a lower one. "Thank you for telling me thy story, my lord."

As the young man exited the Apothecary's shop, another man entered. His face was grim and cold, and his garments black and plain.

"We are closed, good sir," the Apothecary said from across the counter. "You'll have to return on the morrow."

The grim-faced man passed his cold gaze over the empty shop. I am not here for drugs," he said as he picked up a jar of balm. "I am here for money."

The Apothecary crossed his spindly arms. "Well then, what have you to sell?"

"Sell," the grim-faced man said placidly. He set the jar of balm down and faced the old man behind the counter. "I have heard thee to be an alchemist, as well as an apothecary. Is it true?"

"'Tis true," said the Apothecary, with a bit of annoyance.

The black-clad visitor grinned. "I, too, practice the art, though my purpose for it is limited. Observe."

Intrigued, the Apothecary leaned forward as the man stepped closer and produced a small round ball. "This is a special mixture of black powder, Ethiopian gum, and a few other odds and ends. Watch closely."

Casually, the visitor drew his dagger and proceeded to mold the ball about the thin blade. When it was wholly covered, the man asked, "Might I have a lit candle, sir?"

There was a lit candle standing on that very counter. The Apothecary slid it over so it stood between them. With a devilish smile, the visitor placed his dagger o'er the candle's flame. The gum ignited and crackled with green fire and brilliant light.

"Marvelous!" exclaimed the Apothecary with a clap of delight. "I have studi'd to know of such wonders, such works of fire, from the Orient."

In a few seconds, the gum burnt away, leaving only a cherry-red blade.

"And now, to business," the visitor said, the light of the blade reflecting in his large eyes.

"What business exactly, sir? To sell me thy fire-works?"

"No," the visitor replied with a cruel laugh. "My business is to rob you. Come, come! Put all thy money on the counter, and all thy most valuable drugs as well!"

The cherry-red blade ceased to be a wonder and presently became a horror. Trembling, the Apothecary shrank as his boney knees weakened.

"Oh, harm me not! My fortune and goods are thine!"

"The money! Presently!" the robber ordered as he cut and burned away a bit of the old man's beard.

Obediently, the Apothecary squatted down to the shelves beneath his counter.

"Here are my pennies!" he said, placing a large bag up top. "Here are my shillings," he said, placing beside it a smaller bag. "And here, my ducats!" said he, placing up a smaller bag still.

Just before the Apothecary stood back up to face his robber, amongst the many jars, flasks, and clay pots on the shelf, something caught his eye. He snatched it up and stood.

"What is that?" the robber asked, frowning at what the Apothecary held.

In the old man's hands was a ceramic vase shaped like an owl.

60

"'Tis my most valuable substance, at this moment, at least."

"What is it?"

Cautiously, the Apothecary removed the top of the ceramic bird's head.

"Sugar, refined with pig bone and ground to a fine powder. I use it to sweeten my drugs for better imbibing."

"What makes it so valuable?"

The Apothecary laughed nervously. "Well, observe." He took a handful out and tossed it into the air. For a second, it became a cloud of fine dust. Then, either by the lit candle or the glowing knife's blade, the cloud exploded into a ball of fire.

The robber flew back and fell to the floor, his face singed and stern eyebrows obliterated.

Knowing ahead what would happen, the Apothecary managed to dodge the blast and ran to the door that led down to his laboratory. Whimpering and squealing, he descended the steps, pulling his robe up so as not to trip.

"Deceitful swine-son!" the assassino shouted. He rose, dagger in hand, and pursued his mark. "I'll draw thy heart out like the wet head of a half-birth'd babe!" he bellowed down the spiraling steps.

"Henri!" the Apothecary cried when he reached the bottom. Only the hall remained. "Henri!" He ran toward the wooden portal, hands outstretched.

The assassin was closing in fast behind the stumbling old man.

I have him! Valentine thought, raising his dagger for a downward stab.

Just as the assassin drew close enough to deliver a mortal wound, the Apothecary pulled open his laboratory door.

Dozens of sharp fangs surrounding a dark, deep hole flew at the murderous count. It was the last thing he saw and the last thing he felt.

When the unexpected meal was fully devoured, Henri the alligator gazed with appreciation up at the disgusted and trembling features of the Apothecary.

"My massster is kind to me," the alligator said, its glass eyes shining.

The Apothecary winced and withheld vomit. "'Tis a sin to make food of the flesh of man."

"Not for a beassst. There are no sssinsss among beassstsss." Henri's long, flat head tilted, his reptilian features trying to grin.

"Thou art much more than a common beast, Henri," the Apothecary argued before letting out a tired sigh. "I must clean up and close the shop. This…this ugly happening must not become known to the law."

"The law is not thy friend," Henri said, nodding.

"Exactly. No one will miss a common robber, and I've much work to do, much work that the law should not be privy to lest it prevent my redemption."

"Thy brows are join'd in creator's thought, massster," the alligator said. "What is thy plan?"

The Apothecary waved the question away. "I will tell thee after I am finish'd upstairs. I must think on it as I clean. Stay in the laboratory and await my return."

CHAPTER 11
DEATH BY ARPEGGIO

Strutting like a proud peacock, the goat lover made his way down the empty Verona street. Were it not for the darkness of night, his face would be seen as strikingly handsome. He was short, yet well-muscled, with dark brown hair that was nether long nor short.

On he strode without a care, musing o'er his many bestial conquests. Pigs and sheep were among them, yet to him, they paled in comparison to the feel and smell of a female goat in estrus. Since the springtime of his youth, hundreds of goats in Verona did he ravage in secret. No woman e'er brought him the same thrill, the same overwhelming pleasure as that of a goat trapped in his manly grasp.

"Ducy!" a woman's voice called out.

He turned his handsome face to the sound of his name. "How now? Who speaks?"

Rosaline stepped out of the darkness and into the moonlight, a stern beauty in the empty street. "I am the Inquisitor of Verona," she said.

Ducy shook his head and shrugged. "An odd calling for a pretty maid so young," he said with a friendly laugh.

"You think me pretty?"

"Aye, my lady."

Rosaline arched an eyebrow. "Though not as pretty as a goat, at least in thy eyes, yes?"

Startled, the comely man's smile melted like a candle in a forge. "I know not what ye mean," he said.

Rosaline took a step forward. "Thou didst make a drunken confession on a night of revelry. To Friar John thou didst admit to making thyself and half the goats in Verona unclean with thy unnatural lust."

Ducy barely remembered that night. "I was drunk," he defended. "I must have spoken in crude jest. But ho, since when doth Friar John report such things to his superiors? 'Tis a betrayal of the sinner's trust!"

"So, you admit to the sin?" she said, her eyes widening, her plump lips parting into a smile.

Backing away, Ducy cast a hard look at the young woman. "Let me alone, mad woman!" He turned to continue his way down the street but found it blocked by one of Rosaline's tall lictors. The bodyguard's foil was drawn and pointed at the goat lover.

Not lacking for courage, Ducy drew his rapier. His dark eyes glared at the lictor, his strong limbs ready to move and fight. Then, he heard two more swords being drawn behind him. He turned and turned again and saw himself surrounded by three tall, stout men with matching garments and grim bearing. Fear stung Ducy's heart shortly before a razor-tipped point stung his hip.

Yelping, he tried to run and beat away the darting points. He did not make it far. In seconds, he was hunched and kneeling. Every part of him was covered in blood, every part save his sword. The lictors stood about him, their dripping points poised to strike.

Rosaline stepped before him. "Thou art corrupt'd, Ducy. Now is the time to confess."

Despite his pains, Ducy sneered at her in defiance. "I already gave it to the friar, wench!"

He tried to stab her, but a lictor's blade flayed the skin off his wrist. The goat lover's rapier fell as he screamed.

"Confess to thy possession, man!" Rosaline said, her words strengthened by faith and authority. "Did you not tell Friar John that dreams guided thy foul desires? That visions of goats as thou slept did prompt you to couple with them?"

"Aye!" Ducy said, still sneering and clutching his wrist. "But the dreams were born of mine own desire."

"Nay!" the Inquisitor replied. "'Twas the other way 'round. Thy desire was born from those dreams." She looked at him in pity and with disgust. "I see it. I sense it. I know it! Queen Mab hath been with you!"

Ducy shook his head. "Who?"

Rosaline paced around him. "Some good Christians call her a fairy. Heathens would call her a succubus, a fiendish muse spawned from the Devil. For centuries, she has plagued Verona with mischief, madness, and woe. She turns neighbor against neighbor, inspires inventions most unholy, and makes men of weak will fall in love with that which should be left alone. Thou art much like Romeo Montague—fair of face and shagging that which he should not shag."

"You are mad!" Ducy roared as he trembled, cold and stinging. "My crimes may be detestable, but at least I am no murderer like thee and thy heartless brutes!"

Rosaline frowned. "I am sworn to end Queen Mab's evil machinations, no matter the cost, for the good of Verona. Thou hast defiled flesh that was eaten by her subjects. Thou may be absolved due to thy confession. But you are an agent of Mab and must, therefore, die." Her cold eyes yielded to the warmth of sympathy. "I tell thee all this because you deserve to know. Farwell, Ducy."

Frantic, Ducy glanced about at the three lictors. "No!" he cried.

Rosaline raised her chin and addressed her men. "Arpeggio."

One, two, three blades pierced through the body of the goat lover. With each stab, Ducy screamed louder and shriller. Then, he gave up the ghost and the rest of his blood.

CHAPTER 12

THE MADNESS AWAKES

With a wet rag, the Apothecary wiped away old chalk scrawlings on a large slate board mounted to the laboratory wall, making way for new strokes to be made.

Henri crawled atop the lab table to get an easier view. His ridged tail wagged side-to-side as it dangled off the table's edge.

With sharp strokes, the Apothecary listed six names—by each, a cause of death.

-Romeo Montague/Poisoned Heart

-Juliet Montague/Pierced Heart

-Lady Montague/Broken Heart

-Tybalt Capulet/Cut Throat

-Count Paris/Pierced Liver

-Mercutio/Pierced Lung

Addressing the alligator like an apprentice, the Apothecary conveyed his findings and intentions.

"Romeo and Juliet died because I sold him a poison that stopp'd his heart. She, seeing him dead, took his dagger and pierc'd her own heart. Two young hearts destroyed by me. And by me those heart shall be mended. This I vow. The secret love and union of these two hearts did, by ill circumstances, bring about the untimely deaths of the youth's mother and best friend, as well as the young count and Juliet's cousin. Six lives undone."

The Apothecary stroked his scorched beard. "And six deaths will be undone. This I vow. Ignoring law and shunning a hero's renown, I shall bring them all back to life, undoing tragedy and woe with secret deeds and stealthy measures. Three crypts must I visit and corpses disturb. This I vow."

A dark, deep laughter bubbled out of the long beast on the table. "The potion that granted me life—thou shalt employ it for those depart'd as thou dids't for me?"

"Nay," the Apothecary said, shaking his head in slight revulsion. "Thou art a fluke, Henri, though thy accidental resurrection did further my knowledge of the substance's usefulness. Still, I am dismay'd by questions concerning thee. Art thou truly alive? Did the potion fully and truly transform the straw that stuff'd you into bones and organs? Why is it you ne'er defecate? Friar Lawrence was a thick man. And your glass eyes, they seem to be the only thing of yours unchang'd and wholly artificial. Why?"

The beast shrugged with a front paw. "Perhhhhaps because I favor them. SSServe me well, they do. Aye, these are good questions, massster. Would that I hhhad the answer to each. Yet, why dost thou not question my talking to thee?"

The Apothecary scoffed and waved his arms about. "We've been friends for years, Henri. Why would you not talk to me?"

"Indeed!" the beast replied with a monstrous grin. "On with thy plans. Thou hhhast baited me to eagerness."

The Apothecary cleared his throat and pointed at the board with a gnarled digit. "Six distinct causes of death will require six distinct mixtures and applications of the substance. Romeo, Juliet, and Lady Montague's causes were all heart-related, thus requiring similar, and therefore easier, applications. Plunging a deep injection directly into their hearts via the path downward from behind their left collar bones should be the easiest way in."

"Mercutio will require a powder'd form, to be inhal'd through the nostrils. A simple pumping of the chest will allow the corpse to snort the stuff into the damaged lung for optimal healing and resurrection."

"County Paris will be more the challenge, as damag'd livers are not as sackish as lungs. I shalt therefore have to encase his entire liver in a shell of wax before injecting the substance, as to avoid leakage. Would that I had a surgeon to assist me in the extraction and reinsertion of the organ. Still, I think I can manage. 'Twill only require a knife, needle, thread, and a dozen candles. The substance will see to and tend to the rest."

"As to Tybalt, he will be the greatest endeavor. Romeo did cut his throat in a duel, resulting in a complete loss of blood. The wound on the throat can be heal'd by the substance, but fresh blood will I need, and much of

71

it—enough to fill a man. But whence, Henri? Whence and how shall I acquire enough precious heart's blood to fill a man without slaying another?"

"Catsss!!" Henri cried like an excited pupil, his great tail wagging and whipping. "Oh, prithee, use the blood of catsss, massster! They are in abundance hhhere in Verona. There must be hhhundreds, though only twenty or thirty should suffice. And after thou hhhhast drained each one, they can be fed to me for easy disposal. Ohh, on second thought, better it were fohhrty cats, yesss."

Crossing his arms, the Apothecary cocked an eyebrow. "Hmm. Possible it may be, were I to add more foxglove and less ginger. Yes, yes, it could work. If the substance transmogrifies straw to alligator's blood, then why not cat's blood to man's blood?"

The idea grew into a plan, and the man let out a hearty laugh that turned into a mad cackle. "Merry, he who has friends is the most fortunate! Oh, Henri, I see now thy resurrection's purpose! I see now *why* I dreamt up that formula. God is directing me through blessings of knowledge and friendship. He not only shows me a path to redemption, but sainthood itself! My alchemy works more than just wonders, but miracles! Oh, praise God!"

"Yesss!" Henri exclaimed, his glass eyes glowing like embers.

As the alchemist and his familiar laughed beneath the surface of the city, the old man's mind snapped. And to him it felt as blissful a relief as a stiff and weary backbone being popped and cracked in all the right places. All the guilt, fear, desperation, death, discovery, and a single visit from Queen Mab shattered his weak will and ground it to powder. Soon, that powder would meet flame.

CHAPTER 13

CRYPTIC DEEDS

The iron lock was strong and thick,

But with artful fingers-easily pick'd,

Slight of body and light of step,

Into the crypt the Apothecary crept,

With lantern held high he lit the face,

Of the youth he slew in desperate disgrace,

On a bed of stone-under a shrouding net,

Lay the corpses of Romeo and his Juliet,

Their cheeks were pallid-their eyes were sunken,

A fortnight of decay had render'd them shrunken,

Their mouths were open in skeletal yawns,

Long were the teeth from gums withdrawn,

The stench of the lovers on their funeral bed,

Made the man choke and turn his head,

But the lure of success held savory bait,

He went straight to work in the changing of fate,

With a bellows tipp'd with a long bodkin shaft,

He drew in the substance in a single draft,

From a vial mark'd *Romeo*-this substance he drew,

And inserted the shaft between bone and sinew,

Into the heart of the lover who died,

To dwell for eternity alongside his bride,

Next came Juliet for the alchemist's cure,

In went the substance to her wounded heart pure,

When all was done the Apothecary smil'd

Down at the lovers like a father to child,

"Wake up tomorrow to a new day and life

And live long and happy as husband and wife."

◆

Not far from the pair – on a shelf of stone,

Lay Lady Montague resting alone,

A mother robb'd and dealt a hand of grief,

Death had deliver'd her only relief,

For when she was dead she miss'd her son not,

There by his corpse they left her to rot,

The Apothecary spoke as he lower'd her shroud,

76

"Dignified lady – Once wealthy and proud,

God doth not need thee at this present time,

Return with thy children when the dawn bell chimes,

Thy son will be waiting when the new day breaks,

To present a new daughter when thou dost wake,"

He then thrust his bellows sharp – tipp'd like a knife,

Into the heart of Old Montague's wife,

And fill'd every chamber with his substance arcane,

To spread to each organ through dozens of veins,

Thus were his deeds in the Montague crypt,

Before out the door into darkness he slipp'd.

♦

Through a window's iron bars the thin man stepp'd,

Into the crypt of House Capulet,

Hauling three bladders full of stray cat's blood,

With a tilt of his head he threw back his hood,

He look'd round and spott'd the corpse of a youth,

Whose name had been Tybalt – his throat giving proof,

The wound on his neck was deep and clean,

Caus'd by Romeo's rapier long and keen,

With cat gut threads the Apothecary stitch'd,

That mortal wound on the Capulet lich,

The drawing and pumping with his bellows sharp,

Mov'd the cat's blood from bladders to heart,

'Til the body was full of new blood yet warm,

From thirty-five cats bled dry after harm,

The final part came with the substance pour'd,

Upon the stitch'd gash caus'd by Montague's sword,

"I bid thee good night," the old man did say,

"Awake you without any vengeance to pay,

Forgive thy slayer – for now he is kin,

Live not by the sword and you'll live without sin,

Let Tybalt be known as a pacified man,

Reviv'd and redeem'd as part of God's plan."

♦

His last crypt to pry beneath the full moon,

Was the haunt where the nobles all shar'd a tomb,

Stately and grand the edifice rose,

While within past princes lay in repose,

Paris and Mercutio – both noble born,

A brace of kinsmen from Verona's prince torn,

The Apothecary removed the Count's liver with care,

As putrid decay infested the air,

Melting twelve candles with his torch burning hot,

He cover'd the organ – encasing the rot,

Then he injected into the foul mass,

The substance brew'd for this special task,

And as he sew'd the liver back up inside,

Gore and wax on the old man's hands dried,

Yet cared he not for that sickening mess,

For he thought that he'd perform'd a success,

At last came he to the first to die,

Whose death began this tragedy,

Still as stone and white as snow,

In sleeping death lay Mercutio,

"I have heard thee a man of many jests,

Of Romeo's friends-thou art the best,

Return to this world with thy laughter,

I draw thee hence now from the Hereafter,"

With vials full of powder coarse as sand,

He plugg'd up the nostrils of the grave man,

Then with both hands he rhythmically press'd,

Over and over down on the man's chest,

Causing the breath to draw out and in,

'Til all of the powder was inhal'd within.

♦

Thus were his labors under night's cloak,

He made it back home before the dawn broke,

And wash'd his hands clean of deeds and sins,

While six renew'd lives began to begin,

Six separate corpses arose with fresh sense,

And walk'd out the crypts with different intents.

CHAPTER 14

FRIAR JOHN

Friar John rose early to perform his duties, as well as the duties of another friar not to be found. When the church door opened to receive the daily visitors, he saw three tall men armed with foils already standing by his confession booth. He knew those men and dreaded them, yet showed it not when he entered the booth to talk with their mistress.

"Report," came the voice of the Inquisitor.

Friar John shook his head, as if he could feel her stern gaze through the mesh between them. "There is nothing to report, Your Eminence."

"Be there no odd sins or peculiar dreams in the minds or hearts of Verona's subjects?"

The friar shrugged, his eyes blinking and lips quivering. "All sins are odd before the Lord Our God, and the very occurrence of dreams are in themselves peculiar."

The Inquisitor's voice tightened. "Philosophy is for bygone pagan Greeks. Best that you behave like an Italian man of the church, Friar John."

"Aye, Eminence. I will keep that in mind."

There was a pause before the Inquisitor asked "Has Friar Lawrence returned?"

"Nay, Your Eminence. It has been nigh a week, and I fear the worst. The good man has not been the same since the massive tragedy. He gave away all his prized alchemy equipment, all his books and instruments. When a man gives up his mortal joys, he perhaps… Oh, I daren't say it."

"You think he committed suicide? A Franciscan friar and man of the cloth?"

Tears of fear and regret flooded Friar John's eyes. "The tragedy was all my fault, yet he burden'd all the blame. Had I not deliver'd his letter in time, Romeo, Juliet, and Count Paris would all be alive. Yet, Friar Lawrence, in Christ-like fashion, took up all guilt and held me blameless. Oh, but his mind did take a toll. Grief and remorse did break his wits and will. Faith, it would seem that suicide would be his only reason for not returning."

The Inquisitor sighed. "You would know him better than I. I'll have the river and sewers search'd. May God deliver him, in one fashion or another."

"Amen," said the Friar with a whimper.

"So," Rosaline started, changing the subject, "How is our new servant fairing?"

"Well enough. She no longer weeps when she cleans floors, and she hath prov'd a good candle-maker. The vow of silence wears on her though, I can tell."

Something like a small laugh came from the Inquisitor's side. "She was always a gabby woman, though she had no gift for it. Perhaps dipping wicks for hours on end is her true calling."

Friar John frowned in polite perplexity. "Uh... erm... perhaps? Her candles doth burn brighter and longer than past ones use'd."

"Friar Lawrence!" came a voice from outside. "Where is he? Friar Lawrence, 'tis a miracle!"

Both doors of the confession booth burst open as Inquisitor Rosaline and Friar John strode forth into the main church hall. Walking briskly from the entrance came a panting youth not more than fifteen summers old.

"Friar Lawrence! Friar Lawrence!" the youth called as he glanced this way and that. Exuberant joy filled his dark eyes. "Oh, where is he? I must see him!"

"He is not here," Rosaline said firmly, her cold eyes narrowing as she approached the boy. "Who art thou to seek him?"

"Why, it is you, Balthazar, a servant of House Montague," Friar John answered for the boy. "Speak, lad. What is the reason for thy loud joy in God's house?"

"'Tis a miracle!" Balthazar exclaimed, his hands raised in triumphant praise. "They are risen! Cruel death hath lost his hold on they that he took. They are risen!"

"Of whom do you speak, boy?" Rosaline asked, her look betraying annoyance. "Speak plainly, or I will see thee flogg'd."

Balthazar dropped his arms and lowered his head, for although he was brave and strong, he was still a servant at heart. "Pardon me, milady and Friar, for my joy doth make light my feet and judgment. 'Twas this early morn when they came—Lady Montague, Romeo and his new bride, Juliet—all alive as I and thy good selves."

"Alive?" spouted the friar. "But I did help in laying each of them to rest! I have seen enough dead to know dead when I see dead, and they were dead!"

"Yet, now they live," replied Balthazar, who was known to be too stupid to be dishonest.

Rosaline looked to her lictors, who all stood at attention. In the pit of her stomach, doubt churned with fear. She took the cross talisman that hung about her neck and kissed it. "And the dead will rise from their graves," she uttered.

CHAPTER 15

FEAST OF THE RITORNOS

Though sworn to the church with faith of cold iron and a will of tempered steel, Rosaline Capulet was still a mortal maid no more than nineteen years old. The untold volumes of scripture and lore she had read in her raising versed her much in the things of heaven and earth. She had read of miracles and unearthly occurrences and believed in a great many. Yet, to see one affect her own mortal family rang her iron core and chilled her already cold soul.

The home of Montague, thronged by both Montague and Capulet and their servants, was a blubbering, laughing, praising, oath-making scene of mad jubilance and jabbering gaiety. Tears and kisses fell from and upon every face. Arms hugged, hands shook, and many words filled the still cool morning air with sentiments of good will.

She and her lictors stood unnoticed in the feasting hall as the two families, once mortal enemies, conversed and cried and ate in God's honor.

There they were: Romeo, Juliet, and Lady Montague, all alive and hardy in appearance, sitting with Lord Montague, Lord and Lady Capulet, Benvolio, Balthazar, and other members of the two households. All the table was a roar with loud talk.

"Whence came you all?" asked Lady Capulet. "From heaven itself, or were you asleep in death? We saw that dear Tybalt was missing from our crypt, as well, this morning. Oh, I pray he doth find his way here anon!"

"We remember naught save dying and waking in the crypt," Romeo said, his hand clasped with Juliet's. "Yet, I dare say that like heaven this feast doth feel, to be surrounded by so many loves."

"'Tis our wedding feast!" Juliet exclaimed, her pretty features wet with happy tears.

Old Montague, bleary and stumbling, rose from his great seat, his cup held high. "Our houses are one, our fighting is done, and the lord hath return'd our daughter and son!"

Lord Capulet rose with his own cup to add, "Praise to the power of love that is true. It quelleth strife and life renew. Proud I am, through and through, to be father of Juliet Montague!"

All raised their glasses and drank deep. Then Benvolio asked Romeo, "Coz, what didst thou think when you awoke? What was thy first thought?"

Romeo laughed as he chewed a bit of pheasant. "Faith, coz, I did think that Apothecary in Mantua did sell me false poison, and that he had cheated me out of my forty ducats!"

"Peace!" Rosaline cried with bared teeth framed by rose-red lips, and at once the table went quiet.

In his cups, Lord Capulet laughed and addressed the Inquisitor. "Why, there be my holy niece, Rosaline. Come to us, girl. Eat and share in our rejoicing! Since we cannot have God join us at our table to thank, grant us thyself as his representative."

Rosaline raised her chin and approached the table, her beauty augmented by a cold and stately ire. Behind her, the lictors matched her every step. "I come not as thy niece or thy guest. But thou art right and wise to acknowledge me as God's representative."

The lictors, unordered-yet-orderly, paced about the feasting table, surrounding it in even accord with their mistress. The Lords and Ladies, their children and servants, all froze in apprehension.

Rosaline raised her hand, presenting her gold ring bejeweled with a cross of ruby.

"I have no kin here. I have renounc'd all ties and pleasures of the flesh, unlike some." She cast an ill look at Romeo, who promptly turned his worried face to his plate.

The Inquisitor continued gazing at Romeo and Juliet. "The scriptures say that any who committed suicide may not enter the gates of heaven."

Juliet spoke. "Perhaps that is why we were sent back."

"Were every suicide sent back as you were, you little twit, then the world would be full of you... you... *ritornos.*"

Lady Montague raised a finger. "Lady Inquisitor," she started tactfully, "I am prepar'd to answer any question and accept any examination thou dost command, for I am as curious as thou art concerning this occurrence."

Rosaline frowned as if forced to hold bitter wine in her mouth. Looking down at Juliet, she grasped the girl by her long braid and pulled her from her seating place. "Let the inquisition start with this one!" she shouted, drawing a dagger from her hip.

Romeo, his Lord father, and Lord Capulet tried to rise in protest. But all found the razor-edged foils of the Inquisitor's lictors at their throats. With knees half-bent, the three men cowed in sudden fear.

"Don't hurt her!" Romeo cried.

Rosaline paid him no mind as she artfully slashed open the front of Juliet's dress, exposing skin and breasts, but not a drop of blood.

Bursting into tears, Juliet covered herself.

Rosaline yanked the girl's left hand down and pointed at her chest with the dagger, shouting, "Behold! Above her left breast, there should be a scar where she plunged Romeo's dagger. Even Christ had wounds when he rose from the dead. This, this!" She pointed her dagger about the gathering. "This is NOT God's work!"

After shoving Juliet back down to her seat, Rosaline called attention to her lictors. "Come, my men. I do detect the work of Mab here. Her dreams, her lies, and illusions are sweet at first, like this present reunion. But a great evil is afoot. Come now. We've more evidence to uncover."

As the Inquisitor and her lictors sheathed their blades and approached the hall's exit, Romeo stood, his eyes peering, his hand resting on the hilt of his rapier. "Mark me, thou mad woman; touch my love again, and I will surely slay thee—woman or no, Inquisitor or no." He took a step forward, his voice deepening. "I am not afraid to die for her a second time."

Rosaline and her three lictors halted. The men turned, yet the woman remained still. Then the feasting hall filled with something great and terrible: Rosaline's laughter.

"Oh, Juliet," she tittered as she turned. "You should know something about your brave husband."

Juliet, clasping her rent dress together, frowned in attention, her tears still running.

Rosaline spread her arms, her broad black sleeves making her look like a crow in flight. "Not twenty-four hours before he wooed and won thee, Romeo of Montague did seek my hand in matrimony. Imagine how he begged me to turn my back on the church. Envision his weepy bearing as I refused him. Think of how desperately, how poetically he tried to woo me. I sent him hence mewling with melancholy. Think of it this way, you painted twit—he threw his heart at me, and it rebounded off my shield of faith before landing by chance into your perfumed lap!"

Juliet stared off at nothing as the words sank into her brain. Her tears stopped. She addressed her husband. "Romeo, is there any truth in her cruel words?"

With Romeo's courage destroyed, he felt naked where he stood, more naked than Juliet had been just a minute before. He uttered nothing.

All in the hall were silent, and the Inquisitor departed with her men, momentarily satisfied.

CHAPTER 16

RAT AND CAT

Wordless, thoughtless, soundless—the cat stalked the rat in the dark alleyway. The cat had no use for words, for it could not talk a rat into its teeth. The cat had no use for thoughts, for from its birth it knew all it needed to know. And the cat had no use for sounds, for making sounds ruined its hunts and creepings.

The rat, unaware of the cat, gnawed on the bone of a pheasant. The greasy fragment was one of many treasures thrown out of a nearby house. Blissfully, the rat chewed, its busy teeth champing and chattering over any sound the cat could have made.

Closer and closer the cat crept. It knew not that the rat hunting in the city had improved because the cat population was recently decimated by a mad apothecary. The cat only knew that the hunting was good and that the rat's flesh would keep it strong.

After a drawn time of paws creeping and teeth gnawing, the moment came. The cat pounced at the rat, and both animals were doomed.

Snatching the cat in mid-air and the rat from its meat, two hands took up the animals in iron grips. The cat felt fangs upon its neck, and they were not the playful fangs of its past litter mates or the angry fangs of a rival cat, but the hungry fangs of something else. That something bit into the cat's throat and sucked and slurped and drained until the cat was nothing more than a drooping sack of fur with dangling paws.

The rat put up a better fight, scratching and nipping at the hand that held it. But the hand held tight, and a man's mouth opened before the rat. This mouth had no fangs, but a worm-eaten tongue and yellow teeth.

"A plague 'a both their houses," the mouth said as it breathed a yellow cloud of vapor upon the struggling vermin. The rat choked and squeaked as it was forced to breathe in the fetid fumes. Writhing and gagging in nauseous anguish, the small thing perished.

Mercutio and Tybalt gazed at one another in that dark alleyway, each clutching their kill. Tybalt crouched like a lion. Mercutio stooped like a rat. Tybalt's eyes blazed with unnatural red, his needle-like fangs dripping with the cat's juices. Mercutio's eyes were dull and milky white, his skin a pitted and worm infested hide stretched o'er a gaunt frame of bones.

In the cool dark of dusk, the two man-shaped things threw down the dead animals. The cat was the first to arise, its eyes glowing as coals and its tail flickering like a scorpion's tail. When the rat reanimated, its eyes were milky, and yellow puss dripped from its buck teeth.

As the fell creatures scurried off in different directions, a festering Mercutio grinned bitterly at a crouching Tybalt.

"Dark Prince of Cats, when our work in this city is ended, I will see how many ways I can skin thee. And when this time is come, there will be none to stand between us."

Tybalt responded with a low growl that turned into a venomous hiss.

Then, the two fell men parted, in search of more rats and more cats to impart their malign blessings.

CHAPTER 17

A MAN OF WAX

The old woman had spent the entirety of the day downstairs, cleaning Friar Lawrence's now vacant cell. Had she heard the news of Juliet's return from death, the former nurse would have broken her second vow and cried out for joy. Yet, no one bothered to tell her, for none were allowed to talk to her save for brief commands, and her tongue was bestilled by her bitter vow of silence.

The cell was clean, and she, quite dirty. She would have bathed if not for one more duty to perform.

The church slept during that midnight hour. No living thing stirred within it save she. Sore, sleepy, and miserable as only the unloved can be, she trudged her way to her meager quarters. In a basket by her bed were two hundred candles she had crafted herself the day previous. Wincing as she bent, she picked up the basket and trudged, limping and sighing, to the main church hall.

Before the statues of the saints were the melted remnants of two hundred candles lit earlier in wishful prayers throughout the past day. All their lights had dwindled like the joys in her soul. Her heart and soul were utterly beshrewed.

A man stood before the shadowy saints, picking up chips of the melted wax and eating them like sweetmeats. The light of the ensconced torches brought little glow upon his person, yet she could see that he was a tall and well-formed man. This queer sight, obscured as it was, gave her pause.

Though she could have felt fear, she was too simple, too duty-bound to recognize any hint of danger. Setting down her basket, she stomped her foot, clapped her hands, and grunted reproachfully at the man who dared interfere with her last task of the day. Tired and miserable and devoid of patience, all she wanted was to set up the new candles before retiring for the night.

The man turned, his face and garments catching the torchlight. They were fine garments and it, a fine face, a face she knew very well.

County Paris? She thought, her heart jolting to near stillness.

The young count gazed at her as he chewed ravenously on a dwindled candle stick. Smoke wafted from his mouth and nostrils. Hot wax dripped from his mouth like the drool of a hound. His face was smooth and polished with an unsettling texture.

"Juliet?" he said, his lips hardly moving.

The former nurse shook her head and covered her mouth with both hands as she backed away, fear no longer a stranger.

"Juliet…" he said again, moving toward her, his arms stretched out, his mouth panting smoke.

The old woman's muscles seized with panic, causing her to buckle and shrink when she wanted to run and flee.

"Oh! My sweet love! My Juliet!"

As he took hold of her, she broke her vow of silence with a shrieking shout that was quickly stopped by a mouth of choking smoke, scalding wax, and mad desire.

The other servants found her in the morning that followed. Her clothes were torn and rent, her corpse covered in a solid puddle of wax like an unfortunate fly caught in a letter's seal. By her head was her basket, empty save a single candle gnawed to the wick.

CHAPTER 18

AN UNATTENDED SWORD

All of Verona stirred with exuberance from the miracle of the Six *Ritorno*, those who had returned from the dead. Though Tybalt, Mercutio, and Paris were yet to be seen, their resting places were empty, and many people reasoned that the three men would reveal themselves in some grand, yet subtle way, as Christ had done in a garden according to scripture.

Nearly the entire population saw the event as a divine act. Even the man who caused the occurrence believed God was the true orchestrator.

Deep below the Apothecary's shop, the old man sat weeping on his cold, stony floor, his spindly arms about the great neck of his closest friend.

"It is accomplish'd, Henri! Oh, it is accomplish'd!" he said as the raw joy poured out from his wrinkled eyes to fall atop the reptile's flat head.

"Oh, thank God and all the saints, the Son and the Mother!"

"Amen!" added Henri, his mouth opened in a long, sharp grin.

The Apothecary lay his head upon the beast and sighed. "Oh, what wonders we've discover'd. Aye, and what wonders yet uncover'd be. This is only the beginning, friend. From the basic formula of this miraculous substance, I am able to devise variant compounds to overcome the various causes of death. What else is possible through it, ye suppose? I have mix'd and distill'd the nectar of Olympus, the very blood of Christ. The Fountain of Youth springs not from some unexplor'd continent, but from this very laboratory."

"From thy very mind, Massster," Henri said.

The Apothecary yawned as he smiled and did not disagree. His misty eyes twinkled as he mused. "This truly is the Renaissance. All things will be made new again, even those dead before their time. All peoples will live to be old, as I have, that they might live long enough to find redemption, as I have. This is only the beginning, Henri. Only the beginning…"

Heavy lids closed o'er the eyes of the old man as blissful relief bore him away from the waking world and into the oblivious void of dreamless sleep. After a time, Henri slowly opened his jaws and said in a hissing whisper "Hhhe sssleepsss, yet hhhe doth not dream. Come thee hence, my queen."

From under the shut door came the tiny hazelnut carriage driven by the gray-coated gnat and pulled by the team of little atomies. Though the steeds and what they pulled measured no longer than a maid's little finger, Henri' glass eyes saw it clearly as it drew near. The alligator held perfectly still as the carriage rode up his lipless jaws and onto his narrow snout.

Dismounting the driver's seat, the grey-coated gnat shot a grave glance at one of the great monster's glass eyes before opening the carriage door.

Out from that empty shell stepped Queen Mab. Proportioned like a child, yet endowed like a woman, the inheritor of the fairy crown was pretty, despite having a broken and shriveled wing. In her youth, she had been a midwife who guided newborn fairies out of the wombs of poppies and toadstools. Now, all her kind were dead save she, and the crown was hers whether she wanted it or not.

"Is all in disorder?" she asked the alligator, her voice a mixture of polluted honey and corroded bells.

"The fruits of thy labor ripen, my Queen," Henri answered. "The Apothecary's mind is as a fine sword—keen and easily maneuver'd."

"Good," she said, clasping her hands in triumph. "For too long have I waited for such a mind as his! A weak will combin'd with abnormal genius of intellect. Why, even Friar Lawrence never exhibit'd such a rare extreme. A fine replacement this Apothecary is. 'Tis a shame he is so old and with not many years left in him. I should have liked to cause more mischief with him in other cities. Still, I will make of him what I can."

"Shall you give him another dream?" the alligator asked. "He longs to create more miracles."

Queen Mab laughed through closed lips. "If dreams of invention he desires, he shall have them in abundance. I imagine by now his mind is quite broken-in, mushy and comfortable. I will be taking up residence there for the time being." She frowned and sneered. "That she-hound Inquisitor hath been breathing down my neck. She is presently hotter on my trail than any Inquisitor e'er was! I need a place to hide. Even someone as small as I needs places to hide when the eyes of hunters be keen and watchful."

"For how long?" asked Henri.

"Oh, at least until the plan is carried out. Mercutio, Tybalt and Paris are all performing their parts splendidly. Tell me, Henri, how are Friar Lawrence and Count Valentine faring?"

The alligator grinned and laughed lowly. "They are cured and ready, my Queen, and eagerly await their release."

"Good. Keep them waiting. Release them only in a time of great danger or when I bid thee do so."

Just as she turned around to re-enter her carriage, the great reptile stopped her with a last question.

"My Queen, how will I know the difference from when the Apothecary is acting of his own accord and when thou art directing him?"

Mab smiled and waved her hand in dismissal. "Possession is a complicated endeavor to explain, Henri. But if his mind is as you say, an unattended sword, then I'll have little trouble in guiding its keen edge."

She climbed into her hazelnut carriage and bid her coachman to drive. Over the ridged head of the great beast it went, up the sleeping face of the sleeping Apothecary, and the down deep into the hole of his upturned ear.

CHAPTER 19

EXIT ESCALUS

He agreed to meet her by the river. The windy night, starless and moonless, warned of rain brewing in the vast dark cloud above the city. They agreed to meet alone, he without his guards, she without her lictors.

When the prince saw her standing by the water, he could have let himself fall in love, but he knew better. The inquisitors selected for Verona had long been a singular sort: cold in temperament, mechanical in procedure, and ruthless in judgment. He had to remember this was not a mere woman, but an armed right hand of the church itself.

"Prince Escalus," she said as he drew near, not taking her eyes off the water. She raised a hand, which he took to kiss the ring on her finger.

"Your Eminence," he said, shifting his eyes to the water as he stood by her. They were shoulder-to-shoulder and silent as the chill wind flapped their dark cloaks.

"Would that this river were the Jordan," she muttered. "Would that it ran as pure, that the people of this city might be baptize'd anew. Alas, like the streets and roads, it runneth o'er with sin."

"How art thou sure?" the prince asked. "Hath sin a form that only an inquisitor can detect? Doth the seven deadly sins come in seven different colours?" he offered a smile with the jest.

She offered naught but her porcelain mask of an expression. "It hath been three days since thy dead brace of kinsman went missing. The corpses of Mercutio and Paris have vacated their places of eternal rest. And the new count, Valentine, is nowhere to be found." She glanced at him. "And you offer jests. What dost thou know, Prince?"

"Too much and not enough," said he. "Wilt thou hear confession as a priest would, and absolve me of my sins?"

Rosaline smiled. "If I refused you absolution, would you still wish to confess?"

The prince remembered his title then and armored himself with authority and sternness. "What of Friar Lawrence? Why is he absent from this miraculous and holy event? And what of that servant woman found dead in the church? Her name escapes me…"

Rosaline pointed to the river. "At first, methought the ghostly friar might have taken his own life. We expected his corpse to emerge from the river a bloodied mass, but no such luck."

"He might still be alive," the prince offered. "There might still be hope."

Rosaline rolled her eyes and spat into the water. "Hope is not a comfort. Hope is the confusion of absolutes. Hope only prolongs misery. Not knowing, Prince, is man's weakness and therefore, the Devil's strength."

She stepped to him, her face inches from his own. "So, tell me what you know. That is why I asked you here."

The prince steeled himself and spoke. "The abduction of my kinsman's remains concerns me much. Mercutio and Paris were gentlemen. They deserve rest. What concerns me most is not knowing Valentine's whereabouts. I sent him on an errand from whence he never return'd. Before you ask what errand, I will tell thee; Valentine is my family's assassin, my secret weapon in maintenance of power. He did not wish to retire his dagger to become the next count, but fortune made it so. He asked that I grant him one last assassination before retiring to stately duties. He mark'd the apothecary in Mantua who sold Romeo the poison to end his own life, and I gave him leave to slay the man, for the apothecary had broken the law."

Rosaline's eyes widened in apprehension. "Six. Six apothecaries in Mantua were slain recently. All in the same manner. All by the new count?"

"All by Valentine, yes," the prince said with a grave nod. "And yet, the truly guilty one evaded him and reestablish'd his trade here in Verona. I gave him leave to go there, to leave his dagger forever behind in the apothecary's chest. Valentine return'd not. The apothecary still lives."

He sighed and shook his head. "I planned to conduct an investigation, but this... this... miracle happen'd, and I am at a loss on what action to take."

"I suffer no such loss," said Rosaline. "Whilst you and Valentine intrigued thyselves with bloody exploits, a terrible power has grown in our fair city. Concern thyself not with the dealings of wretch'd apothecaries and their suicidal customers. Queen Mab is planning something catastrophic, something most diabolical. I must conduct a city-wide inquisition."

The prince scoffed and paced about, his black cloak flapping. "Fie! Again with this Queen Mab! Mercutio would oft talk of her in his mad ramblings. She is a myth, to be sure, a myth and nothing more!"

Rosaline raised her chin. "The inquisition I propose shall determine that, good prince. The Vatican will grant me leave to conduct the affair, but only if thou dost agree to it. I need every person, man, woman, and child, dragg'd out of every house and edifice. I need them, pacifi'd, and processed through the city square where I will put each through a series of tests and inspections. A papal army can arrive in but three days to assist us if you but only agree to my council."

The prince closed his eyes and balled his fists. "All I ever wanted was peace in Verona's streets! You dare ask otherwise? What proof you of the fairy demon queen's existence?"

"The *ritornos*," she said plainly.

"The *ritornos*?" the prince said with a sour grimace. "The resurrection of Romeo and Juliet have brought nothing but joy to the city. God was merciful and return'd them."

"And what of thy kinsman, Escalus? What of Tybalt, my brother-in-flesh? They are still missing."

The prince had no answer, no words.

The Inquisitor placed a hand on the prince's arm. "We both want to know, Escalus. We both feel the pang of not knowing. For too long, the Inquisitors of Verona have been forc'd to hunt that unholy bitch using discretion and secrecy. For too long, has she sewn her seeds of strife in the dreams of our people. She is a lying muse, a succubus, a misleader of the hearts of men. The dreams she inspires turn friends to enemies and enemies into lovers and lovers to corpses all for one goal—our spiritual annihilation, to destroy our peace."

Prince Escalus crossed his arms and gazed upon the passing waters. Even in moon and starlight, it always looked black. Even when the sun shined upon it, it reflected little light. He spoke. "Valentine was a good boy, mother's favorite. His gentleness rival'd Saint Francis himself. But when manhood drew upon him, he would dream of slaying men. The dreams persist'd until the desire to fulfill them took root in his soul. Slaying became his only joy and greatest talent. Rather than condemn him, we put him to use." He paused and shook. The faces of Valentine, Paris, and Mercutio—his last remaining kin—

flashed before his eyes. A fit of grief overtook him, and he crouched to weep upon the dirty street.

"I was not afforded time to even mourn them!" he cried. "First, Mercutio was taken, but I had to dispense justice in place of tears. Then Paris was slain by the same man I banish'd. And now, oh now! Now, that same Romeo is newly alive. What right have I under heaven's gaze to condemn a man who God did return?"

Rosaline stood over him. "God did no such thing. The judgment thou pass'd was a righteous one. Romeo deserv'd death then and still doth! I would run my tests on these ritornos. Let me prove them unholy. My methods are sanctioned by his Holiness, the Pope. My knowledge and trainings are derive'd from the findings of the last twelve inquisitors.

"For too long hath Queen Mab surviv'd in the guise of rumor and myth. She hath been sighted again and again by many a light sleeper."

"Madness!" the prince protested.

"Mercutio saw her once!" Rosaline protested. "He tried to tell others, but none ever believ'd him. People thought him a mad jester, but not I!"

"Stop this at once!" ordered the prince. He stood and wiped his wet cheeks. "I will have order. I will have peace. I will not have my citizens brutaliz'd and torn from their comforts. My streets will remain pacified places. Keep thy inquisitions private, Rosaline. If ill matters come about, then I shall deal with them as they come."

"Thou art a fool!" Rosaline shouted, her perfect teeth clenched.

The prince sneered at the insult. "And thou art a woman. You belong in a convent, not the high office of Inquisitor."

"Ah," Rosaline said, suddenly becoming eerily calm. "So, it comes to that. I am to be ignor'd like Cassandra, who only wish'd her city's salvation. So be it, Escalus. Thou hast proven to me thine inherent foolishness. Foolishness kill'd thy kinsman, Mercutio and Paris. Perhaps even Valentine brought death upon himself by dancing with death."

"I do not dance," said the prince, his eyes matching hers in coldness.

Rosaline frowned, as if mildly disappointed. With a shrug, she turned and began to walk away.

"You are a mad woman, Rosaline Capulet," the Prince called out to her. "As mad as thou art beautiful, I dare say."

She turned, her arms crossed, her face cold and serene. "I see the chaos for what it is. What you call madness, I call a reason'd fear. Good night, Escalus. I will pray that thy poor judgment will not doom us all."

On the way back to his palazzo, Prince Escalus of Verona stopped by his family crypt to mourn and to think. A chill hour passed as he sat on a stone bench, thinking of his missing kinsman. When the icy rain came, he took refuge inside the crypt. Surrounded by the bones of his ancestors, he knelt and prayed for answers.

As he prayed aloud for guidance, a shadow-clad rat scurried up to him and bit him upon the knee. More frightened than hurt, he ran out of the crypt and through the pouring rain.

When he arrived home, his knee throbbed, his joints ached, and his head pounded like a church bell. Shivering, he climbed into bed, blaming the rain for his sickness.

"I must rest," he thought as he closed his eyes. "Perhaps I am a fool, and the Inquisitor is right. I must sleep on the matter."

By morning, his worries were ended. He was dead.

CHAPTER 20

THE LAST DOSE

The internment of the prince's bones was attended by all of Verona's noblest daughters and sons. Among them: Old Montague, Lady Montague, their son Romeo, and Romeo's wife Juliet.

Friar John deliver'd the eulogy. From a boldly scrawled manuscript, he thus read:

"Lord, grant him mercy, for he was merciful in his justice. Lord, satisfy his thirst and hunger for righteousness, for he was a righteous prince."

"Hmph," Romeo scoffed under his breath. "I aveng'd his kinsman, and for that, he banish'd me."

Juliet rolled her eyes. "And all you did was cut my cousin's throat." Her words dripped sarcasm like blood from a sword.

Romeo looked at her, his face puzzled and concerned. "Love, did you not pardon me for that offense on the night of our consummation?"

"Aye," Juliet said, her face and voice calm. "And since you acknowledge now that it was an offense and not an act of justice, you can hardly blame our depart'd prince for banishing thee."

Shaking his head and blinking, Romeo's words were made to follow a pause of confusion. "Love, art thou still anger'd with me about Rosaline?"

Juliet held her tongue, and with it, Romeo's stones.

"Speak," Romeo said, half-begging, half-demanding.

"Peace!" Lady Montague told them in a shrill whisper. "I'll have no more quarrels betwixt the two of thee. Lord husband, tell these children to—" her words halted when she beheld her husband, forward slumped and sleeping. "Husband!" she hissed, nudging him hard with her elbow.

Bleary-eyed and flatulent, Old Lord Montague woke with a start. "Oh!" he cried. With the luck of Felicitas, none heard him over the crowd of mourners. "What now?" he asked, looking at his scowling wife.

"Thou art influenc'd," she said, her bearing grim.

"Influenc'd, sweet wife? What meanest thou?"

"Thou knows what I meanest, thou fat lout. Thou art still using that drug Benvolio procurr'd for thee. You need it no longer, husband! Thy wife and son are alive."

Old Montague shrugged awkwardly, his eyes falling to the floor. "And for that I am joy'd evermore. It's just, the drugs were of great expense, and 'twould be a waste to waste them."

Juliet turned to face her father-in-law. "I heard that you promis'd in the prince's presence to make a statue of me of pure gold. How can you keep such a promise when spending the family fortune on drugs?"

Lady Capulet glared in shock at the young lady. "Thou truly art kin to Rosaline and Tybalt Capulet. Thy tongue is sharp, girl, and edg'd for quarreling."

Romeo raised an eyebrow and grinned. "Fear not, mother, for I shall dull that tongue with many kisses e'en if it take me constant application of the deed."

Juliet groaned as she sat back in the pew and crossed her arms. "My only hate, sprung from my only love, too long kept hid below now display'd above."

Old Montague managed to stay awake throughout the service's remainder, though he spoke little with the other nobles in attendance. All he desired was sleep, better to avoid the constant bickering betwixt his wife, son, and daughter-in-law. All his thoughts gravitated to the drug crafted by the new apothecary in the city.

Though Benvolio had warned him not to abuse the drug, the hungry gulch that was the old man's grief had driven him to habitual practice. Addicted and enslaved, not even the joy of loves to life returned could free him from the drug's fettering hold.

Once returned home, he took refuge in his private chambers and ordered none to disturb him until supper. After locking the door and opening a window for fresh air, he retrieved a small pewter box from a small chest on a small table. From that box he plucked one of several sticky balls. Placing the ball beneath his tongue, he sat in his comfy old chair and waited. The wait was not a long one, for as the ball dissolved, so too did the old man's concerns. The sweetest of soothing sensations from within caressed his every nerve. Every tense sinew in his blubbery being calmed like a warm wildfire. With present worries now quelled, he commended his mind and spirit to the warm honey oblivion of sleep.

Slumping in his chair, his heavy head fell to one side. A fresh stream of drool oozed from his mouth, and all his wits were as dull as a column.

The cat landed noiselessly upon the window sill. It was a pretty calico pussy with a rich and full coat of fox orange, thundercloud black, and snow white. The coat was flawless save a matted crust of dried blood about the animal's throat. In place of long black pupils in its eyes, two slits of luminous red.

With no consideration for privacy, the small feline entered the chamber and leapt atop one of Old Montague's knees. The man stirred, groaned, and again went still. Carefully, the cat climbed to the summit of the lord's globous belly. Once there, it stood on its hind legs and placed its front paws upon Old Montague's neck. Nipping and tearing a small hole in the drugged sleeper's neck, it suckled the well-placed wound as a kitten suckles its mother. Pressing and kneading with its paws against the fat throat, the cat closed its eyes and purred in ecstasy as it nursed the civil blood.

Old Montague was still alive when the fiendish ca. had drunk its fill and departed from whence it came. But the blood kept coming out, drenching the man's fine clothes and the cushions on which he sat. He never felt a thing. Ever again.

CHAPTER 21

AMBITION AND ARDOR

The moment she had laid eyes upon the dead prince, Lady Capulet was overcome with lust. The funeral was for her pure torture. She longed throughout the service to return home with her husband to join loins for a night of wanton celebration.

She had loathed Prince Escalus ever since he had passed the judgment that her nephew's murderer be banished and not hunted down. She resented the fact that Romeo was alive and well whilst Tybalt, risen or no, was still missing. She saw the prince's untimely death as an act of divine retribution. And she, being in her own mind a pious woman, wished to thank and praise God by aid of her husband's manhood.

Throughout the funeral service, she whispered things into her lord husband's ears, things she wanted to do to him and things she would have him do to her. Kindling and stoking his ardor was no difficult task for he, too, was glad the prince was dead. Lord Capulet saw the absence of Count Valentine and the demise of Escalus as a means to advance his family. The prospect of seizing control of Verona titillated his fancy to an obscene degree. Gifting his daughter Juliet's hand to Count Paris, at the time, seemed the only and best way to acquire a portion of that royal power. But now, with that whole family dead, it did seem that all sovereign power was there for the taking.

When the Lord and Lady arrived at their handsome palazzo that crisp evening, Lady Capulet dismissed all the household's servants for the night.

"I plan to teach the banshees how to wail this night," she whispered to her husband as they ascended their grand staircase. "I want thee to ravish me by candlelight!"

"As you command, my love," the old lord said with a wicked grin. "For tonight, I will play the part of Theseus, and thou shalt play Helen!"

The lady returned the grin. "Helen, I shalt begin to play, but by night's end my role wilt change to that of Venus!"

When they arrived into their bed chamber, Lady Capulet had to stave off her husband's advances for she saw that something was amiss.

"My candles!" she cried. "All my glorious candles. Where have they gone?"

All about the large and comfortable bed stood several candle stands, each one empty.

"I wanted candles!" the lady groused, balling her fists and stamping her foot.

Lord Capulet pawed and caressed his wife as to urge her to forget. She pushed him away and sat on the bed, arms crossed.

"Those lazy servants! How dare they forget to put new candles in our bedchamber?"

"Fear not, wife," Capulet said, frowning and fidgeting. "There are sure to be more candles in our home. I will go and fetch some, and all will be well." He smiled, eyes full of worry and hope.

The lady sighed and gave a bored nod. "Very well. Do hurry."

Hurry he did, as fast as his legs could carry him. He first checked the chambers that had been Tybalt's, and no candles did he find. He then check'd the former chamber of his daughter, and no candles did he find. He check'd the chambers of his servants, and no candles did he find. Minutes passed as he searched his palazzo's inner immensity. At last, defeated and fruitless of his labor, he returned to his bedchamber empty-handed. The room was dark, save for the faint light of a crescent moon glinting through the opened window. With eyes shocked by darkness, Lord Capulet saw the smooth outline of his wife on their bed. She was naked, fair as day, and spread like a dove in flight.

With his lust and confidence renewed, he threw off his robes and joined her atop the mattress. He wasted no words, no time, and took his wife in a passionate embrace, kissing her and entering her all at once. His tongue and manhood burned with passion, burned with lust, burned with…hot wax…

Screaming in pain and horror, Lord Capulet rolled off the corpse, off the bed itself. Gripping his scalded crotch and spitting out bits of wax, the lord writhed and shrieked upon the chamber floor. Scrambling to his feet, he stood and looked upon the atrocity in his bed. He could see it all now in the pale light of Diane's orb—his bed, his dead wife, covered in patches of dried wax. Her nose, mouth, and womanhood drizzled the molten substance. On her face, a frozen look of terror and revulsion.

Mad with grief and fright, Lord Capulet screamed long and loud into the night, teaching the banshees to wail.

When his servants returned the next morning, they found him naked and wielding his long sword in the palazzo's entry corridor.

"Which of you did it?" he asked as he cleaved into the group of them. "Which of you foul fell fiends did it?"

By the time a troop of town guards could be summoned to subdue the madman, Lord Capulet had already hacked three of his servants to pieces.

CHAPTER 22

THE EYES OF HENRI

Through orbs of glass a gypsy lass,
Can glean all things unseen,
For crystal balls reveal all,
That will be and has been,
With bell and book they learn to look,
And spy with trained eye,
Even events that are present tense,
Their sense of sight doth fly,
But eyes of glass see twice as fast,
With clarity wrought two-fold,
No wall or roof can hide a truth,
From what glass eyes behold,
How that lizard was like a wizard,
With such a sly persona,
Through the city's maze he'd cast his gaze,
To every corner of Verona.

In the solitary darkness of the Apothecary's laboratory, Henri the Alligator was seldom bored. For in the cursed city of Verona, there was always a sight to intrigue or entertain him.

On this night, such sights were many.

He saw Lady Montague, Romeo, Juliet, Benvolio, and all the remaining servants of House Montague and House Capulet gathered in the Montague palazzo. All wore black and grieved as though the sun and stars themselves had died. Young Romeo's face was an amalgam of rage and stricken sadness. He drew his rapier and held it high, calling everyone's attention. He gave an impassioned speech, and all the men drew swords to raise with his. Then men each took a turn to kiss Romeo's hand as a sign of loyalty, for he was now Lord Montague. Henri the Alligator was sure to count each sword.

Elsewhere, the reptilian monster saw Inquisitor Rosaline by the city gates. To one of her stern-faced lictors she gave a sealed letter. The bodyguard knelt, kissed her ring, and made a solemn oath before riding out of the city on a fleet-hooved stallion.

Henri then shifted his supernatural gaze onto Tybalt. The Dark Prince of Cats stalked yet another stray cat in a shadowed alley. With low cunning and unnerving speed, the ritorno caught the small beast and drained its blood. In little time, the cat rose to seek out fresh blood for its own consumption. So far, nearly a third of the city's cats were thus turned.

Mercutio roamed the subterranean sewers, exalting his putrid breath in the form of yellow mist. Every rat he passed gagged on the smoky clouds of diseased fumes. Some died within minutes, others hours, but all would rise with the sole and soulless purpose of spreading Queen Mab's plague.

Wax-skinned Paris moved unheard and unseen to every home and building, stealing and devouring every candle he could find. The wax melted into liquid inside his fire-hot stomach and loins. Whenever he ate his fill, woe and doom came to any woman nearby that rekindled his broken memories of Juliet, his once betrothed. In life,

County Paris was a man of honor, tenderness, and virtue. But as a risen ritorno, he was but a puppet in an evil induction.

Through the cats, rats, and missing candles, the people of Verona were losing blood, health, and convenient light when fell things crept and crawled in night's cloak. For Prince Escalus, Old Montague, and Lady Capulet were not the only victims of Queen Mab's silent attack.

No beds were safe. The rats and cats invaded both cradle of babe and cot of slave, from the bedchambers of the prettiest maiden to the stained sheets of the foulest whore, from the most learned scholar to the bravest soldier. By the night's end, a third of Verona would be dead or dying.

The last place Henri looked was the shop above. There, the Apothecary stocked his shelves with dozens of small glass vials, each one containing a dose of his latest alchemical creation. The old man's face was a tittering mask of mad glee. The Queen steered him, seducing his mind with the promises of divine rewards and cosmic truths to be uncovered. Like a subtle arcane muse, Queen Mab inspired lies of the sweetest deceit.

When, at last, the morning came, a crowd of hundreds spewed through the shop door. All had suffered weakening bites of rats and cats throughout the night. Many of them had even dropped dead on the way to the Apothecary's shop. All looked on the brink of death, as though they were on deaths' doorstep and not the Apothecary's.

The old man received the ailing throng with the utmost courage and social grace. To many of them, he gave a vial of his substance, whether they had money or not. And with it came the promise of curing salvation. Indeed, when each person had drunk their prescribed dose, the anemic effects of blood loss and the feverish effects of plague at once vanished from their beings.

Alas, the Apothecary had only a few dozen vials in stock and just as many would-be patrons perished, bawling in front of the shop's closed door.

CHAPTER 23
COUNCIL OF SALVATION

For three horrific nights and three lamentable days, the people of Verona diminished in number and in resolve. The rats beplagued each they bit—man, woman, and child. The cats nursed blood from the necks of the weak and invalid, from infant and infantile. Every candle in the city disappeared, making the task of biting a person all the easier for the nocturnal monsters.

The crypts and public mass graves ranneth o'er. Corpses late discovered stank up streets and buildings alike. Death visited every family and household whilst his sister, Despair, visited nearly every heart.

With the demise of Prince Escalus, the small army of Verona relinquished command to the Inquisitor. On all sides of the church, and in every hallway within, soldiers stood in rigid lines, outwardly vigilant, inwardly restless, for even among their own number the rats and cats made victims. Thus fortified, Rosaline issued her three lictors to seek out and deliver three particular men for a council of salvation.

In her book-laden study with walls bedecked with charts of strange geometry, she sat waiting behind her writing table, praying.

"Our Father, who art in heaven, grant the three men I summon today the wisdom to obey my orders. Grant my lictors speed to bring these men, for I am not a patient inquisitor. A patient heart lacks initiative. And what I lack in patience, I do surely make up for in initiative. Let this meeting render up the secrets of this great evil and the answers with which to quell it. Amen."

Just as she finished, a voice from without announced presence.

"My Lady Inquisitor. 'Tis I, Guiducci. I have brought the Herald to speak with thee."

"Enter," she replied, standing.

Through the chamber door came her lictor. Behind him, an enormous man bearing a magnificent halberd. His short-cropped beard and long mustachios formed a blond capital 'A' below a pair of eyes of the coolest blue. His helmet was a burnished beacon of war-like authority. His armor, though light, fit his perfectly formed shoulders and broad chest as if it were a second skin.

Rosaline raised her chin and smiled as she met the tall man's gaze.

"Greetings, Herald. Verona bleeds for salvation. I thank our Holy Father He hath sent it in the form of thee and thy fellow soldiers."

The Herald bowed, and in a thick Swiss accent, he replied, "The Papal Army you requested is but a league hence, Inquisitor. We are five hundred in number and ten thousand in strength."

The Inquisitor arched an eyebrow. "Do explain the mathematics of thy words, sir, for I follow thee not."

"What I mean is that we are five hundred soldiers, and each soldier, my fellow countrymen all, are worth twenty of thy local guard."

Rosaline nodded. "The blessing of the Pope imparts great power."

The herald grunted in the negative. "More like the Pope's blessing allows great power. Mistake us not for a legion of paladins or crusaders. We are professional mercenaries, handsomely paid, and with no less honor or loyalty than a knight pledged to a lord's service. Our homeland's soil makes for poor tilling, so we have instead master'd the arts of tilling the bodies of men with pike, halberd, and partisan. I tell thee this, of course, with all due respect to thy divine office, Inquisitor."

Rosaline frowned as she weighed the herald's words. Holding up her ringed hand, she asked, "Will you kill any and all without question? There are fell magics and witchcrafts ruining the bodies and souls of my city. Will you slay all those I deem corrupted, be they women or even children? Be they half the population of Verona if need be?"

The massive herald leaned forward, his mouth inches away from her hand. "The Papal Army is a sword for the Pope to wield and direct. He hath handed it off to thee, Inquisitor. What necks thou dost put its edge to is thy business." He kissed the ring, and Rosaline smiled darkly.

"My Lady Inquisitor," came another voice from without.

"Enter."

In came a second lictor, and behind him, Lord Romeo of House Montague. The fair-faced youth looked hardly a youth at all, as though the springtime of youthful happiness were decades behind him and seas beyond him. His eyes were dark with circles, his knuckles white from clenched fists, and his gait was a methodical, stalking one.

With words dripping contempt, yet restrained in temperance, he said, "Inquisitor Rosaline, what mean you by this summons? My men need me. This city needs me and my men. Together, we have already rooted out hundreds of rats and cats. My sword will not be satisfied until every devilish pest in Verona lies in twain."

Rosaline scoffed and crossed her arms. "I've heard of your recent exploits, Romeo. Since thy father's death, thou hast led thy men and the men of House Capulet on a vigilant quest of hunting nobility. I commend thee, young lord, for slaying so many vampiric cats and diseased vermin. But such efforts, I fear, are in vain."

"It hath only been three days," Romeo said, biting the air.

"And still, our numbers dwindle. No. Thy thirst for vengeance shall not be quench'd by such a petty method. You've more sense than Lord Capulet, though, I'll give thee that."

Romeo sneered and shook his head. "Lord Capulet, my poor father-in-law, hath no sense—not anymore. The phantom wax ravager committed lethal violence on his wife. I blame him not for going mad. Speak no ill of the man, I pray you."

The Inquisitor tilted her head and addressed the huge Swissman in the room. "Herald, I did request from the Pope a certain document, a form most official. Do you have it with you?"

"I have," said the herald, producing and handing her a rolled and sealed parchment.

Rosaline took it and promptly handed it to Romeo. "Give this to Juliet. It is for her eyes only."

Romeo took the parchment and stuffed it into his frilled shirt. "This is why you summoned me? Thou couldst have given this to my manservant to deliver."

"I need you here," she said simply.

"For what purpose?"

"For an answer."

"To what question?"

"My Lady Inquisitor," came the voice of the third lictor from without the chamber.

Rosaline smiled and clapped her white hands in delight. "Thou art about to find out, Lord Romeo. Enter, good lictor!"

The third lictor entered. Behind him, a man that Romeo recognized with a look of shock of wonderment.

"You!" the young Montague exclaimed.

The Apothecary regarded the flabbergasted youth with a serene and dignified air, as though he were a king acknowledging the presence of an acquainted subject. Smiling thinly, the old man nodded to Romeo before addressing the Inquisitor.

"Your Holy Eminence, I come at thy calling. How can this bent and humble man serve thee and thy glorious church?"

Rosaline uttered not a word until the old man kissed her ring. "Like a sail catches wind, so, too, do I catch wind of rumors. Great evil has befallen the city I hold dear. The Inquisition begins this day, this very moment, in this very room. Tell me, Apothecary, the plain and simple truths I demand. Leave out no detail, employ no charm of speech nor trick of diplomacy. Render me the answers I seek, for thy very soul is being weigh'd and measured in this most dire of moments.

The Apothecary sighed deeply, almost shrugging as he did so. "My lead-laden conscience doth reach to thy wise judgment, Inquisitor. My heart is sick and sore with secrets. Ask thy questions. And if my answers displease thee and bring about my condemnation, then I will at least die an honest man."

Rosaline sat, glancing back and forth between the Apothecary and Romeo. "Didst thou e'er meet this youth in Mantua?"

"Aye. Some few weeks pass'd."

Didst thou sell him a drug, a poison strong enough to slay a man within seconds?"

The old man nodded, frowning. "Aye, I did. Had I known he would use it to slay himself, I would not—"

"Peace!" ordered the woman in black. She shifted her cold gaze to Romeo. "Lord Montague, doth he speak true?"

"He doth," answered Romeo, his shock now settled to bemused puzzlement.

The Inquisitor addressed the old man. "The penalty of selling such drugs is death." She let the words linger in the air. "But, at present, there is too much death going around—too much or not enough. Apothecary, do you know why I am not ordering my lictors to skewer thy torso with their foils?"

The Apothecary stooped in submissive surrender, yet his face betrayed no hint of fear or worry. "My Lady Inquisitor, both you and the Lord seem to work in mysterious ways. Perhaps that is why he made thee his instrument. I venture no guess as to why thou dost withhold justice."

"Because I live once more!" Romeo answered boldly. "When he did sell me that poison, he did condemn himself by the law's standards. But when St. Peter did turn me hence from heaven's gate and return'd me and my loves to life, this poor old man's sin was purg'd. With crime and sin undone, so to should be penalty. I yet live, therefore, so should this man."

Rosaline rested her delicate forehead upon her palm, rolled her doe eyes, and scoffed. "Romeo, thou fool of fools. Keep thy tarnish'd tongue of silver press'd to thy mouth's roof. Not everything is always about thee."

She turned her attention back to the Apothecary. "A score of citizens hath testified before me and my subordinates that thou didst cure them with powerful remedy. Thus far, no treatment but thine seems to quell the plague. Are these testaments true?"

"Aye, Your Eminence," the Apothecary said, raising his posture back to a stately air. "'Tis within my knowledge to distill an extract to which any ill can be cure'd. Six and thirty doses had I on hand when the plague erupt'd, and just as many sufferers did it bring salvation."

Rosaline arched an eyebrow, her brown eyes glinting. "Have you anymore doses? If not, can you make more?"

The old man spread his frail hands. "Alas, all that I had was used that morning, and with the city being seal'd off to contain the plague, I've no means to acquire the exotic ingredients needed to produce the drug."

Swift as Diane's arrow, Rosaline produced quill, ink, and parchment.

"What are these ingredients? I can secure them for thee with utmost haste. If you can save the city, the church wilt surely offer thee pardon for thy fatal crime.

133

And with that pardon will come wealth beyond thy wildest—"

She paused, put down her quill, steepled her fingers, and narrowed her gaze.

"Wait now," she said in low and studious suspicion. "Tell me, Apothecary, how didst thou come to create this miracle potion that cures all ills?"

The Apothecary seemed puzzled by the inquiry. "By the same proven methods any man of the art would put to use. Trial and error, Platonic reasoning, scientific analysis. All these things I did employ. The substance is the result of a lifetime's worth of work." He pointed to Romeo. "And were it not for this lad's forty ducat payment, I would not ever have procur'd the shop and ingredients need'd to uncover my discovery."

He bowed to the young lord, adding, "I never thanked thee, Romeo Montague. You not only saved me from the pangs of poverty and famine but perhaps the whole city by relation of our dealing."

Romeo could not help but smile. "Well, thou was a near skeleton last I saw thee, good sir. Certainly, now thy old bones bear the weight of fruitful success."

The Apothecary laughed and patted his swollen middle. "Aye, my lord! And sweet success it hath been!"

"Enough!" Rosaline said, pointing her quill at the parchment. "Tell me what you need, what the city needs."

The Apothecary grinned with mad focus and gleeful eagerness, causing the Inquisitor of Verona to flinch in apprehension to this sudden change of expression.

He told her what he wanted. She wrote it all down. And deep within the brain of the Apothecary, Queen Mab laughed with cruel delight.

CHAPTER 24
EXIT JULIET

"Do not leave me here!" Juliet pleaded to her husband as he donned his black cloak.

"Fear thee not, love," Romeo insisted. "For every rat and cat in this palazzo is vanquish'd and discard'd without. Every hole and crevice from which they crawl'd hath been patch'd with mortar and pitch. Thou wilt be safe here as I lead our men on another nocturnal hunt. Again, love, fear thee not."

"'Tis not that," Juliet said with a shake of her pretty head. "I cannot endure thy mother any longer. She was ever the bitch before her husband died, but now that widowhood is upon her, her every word is demand and her every action is punishment! Oh, Romeo, treat me!"

Romeo ran stiff fingers through his soft wavy locks, fighting the urge to uproot them all. "Oh, give her pardon, girl. At least she did not take a long sword to her servants when finding her spouse murdered. She is not half as mad as he! Peace now, girl, and let me save our city!"

Juliet stood up from their bed, her face beaming with contempt. "My father was already a madman, and my neglecting mother, no better! At least, I have the sense to hate them as you should hate thy overbearing mother."

Romeo but scoffed and sighed as he buckled his sword belt.

Juliet crossed her arms and paced about her husband, her eyes burning with scorn. "I can see it now—now that I've lived with both thee and her. 'Twas thy mother that made you such a fawning, lack-will'd, narcissus."

Romeo met the eyes of his wife with grim bitterness. "What dost thou mean?"

She pushed him back, her dainty hands slapping sharply into his chest. "I mean that, to you, I am nothing more than a clear pool of water, a mirror to reflect thy own pitiable vanity. You desire not love from a woman—not truly—but merely thy own love reflect'd back to thee! Thy sickly neediness and thirst for my affections is but vanity at the expense of mine own heart and body!"

"I died for thee!" Romeo shouted down in her face.

Juliet laughed. "Thou wouldst have surely died for Rosaline—for any girl—had she accepted thee. For how is life worth living without a figure of doting motherliness that thou can cleave into with thy vain lust and boyish clinging?!"

He struck her, and she fell to the hard stone floor, her cheek burning with the heat of the blow.

Instantly, Romeo was kneeling by her side, blubbering and begging pardon. Her pounding ears drank his many words, yet her stunned mind heard them not.

She felt herself picked up and gently placed upon the bed. There, Romeo held her and wept into her bosom for several minutes. She moved not a fiber in her being, uttered not a sound. Eventually, after more mewling for forgiveness, Lord Romeo took his leave of her, promising that all will be well again once he and his men brought salvation to the city.

When Juliet arose from her bed, her eyes slowly shifted to the letter on the small table by the shuttered window. Romeo had set it there prior to their conflict. He had told her that Rosaline gave it to her—a letter from the Pope of Rome himself—for her eyes only.

Stepping like a wary thief, she approached the letter. The wax seal was stamped like a coin, displaying the regal profile of the pontiff. She picked up the letter, took a deep breath, and snapped that face in twain.

When first she read the letter's contents, she did not know what to think or feel. When she read it a second time, she felt a spark of hope glimmering in her shadowed heart. When a third time she read it, she wept with such joy and relief that it took all her will to stay silent.

Doffing her noble gown, she stood naked before her vanity mirror. From the upmost drawer she drew out a dagger, long and sharp as a razor.

Oh, happy dagger, she thought, giggling to herself.

With spirited glee, she cut a part of her that Romeo held dear, a part that he loved to kiss and caress endlessly. The blade slashed and tore without mercy, until her long,

139

black braid fell like a flowing garment to the floor. Thus hastily groomed, she donned a suit of Romeo's clothes, a dull-colored outfit fit for travel, and gathered up all the money and jewels held within that master bedroom.

After leaving the pope's letter open upon the bed, she stepped out into the hall, careful to steal quietly. Night had fallen, and there were no candles to light her way. So, she took a burning torch from the wall and padded softly down the hallway. Many of the servants would either be asleep or out hunting with their lord. Her only concern was sneaking past Lady Montague's room without being detected.

When the lady's door came to view, no light shined from within.

She is surely sleeping, Juliet thought, hoping and dreading.

Her heart pounded in her chest as she tip-toed past the sealed portal. The stairway leading down to the main hall was but thirty paces away. From that main hall, it was but a short sprint to the palazzo's main entrance.

Just as she moved past Lady Montague's door, it opened, and Juliet froze in panic. Turning around and lifting her torch, she expected to see the glaring face of her mother-in-law. Instead, she beheld the wide-eyed visage of County Paris.

"Juliet!" he exclaimed as melted wax spurted from his nostrils and manhood. The young count was naked and covered in patches of dried wax, his hair clumped in the substance. His glossy blue eyes were fixed still and unblinking.

Juliet, too frightened to scream, ran to the marble steps leading down. Her torch blazed like a shooting comet as she dashed. Waxy fingers grasped at her hair, but he was unable to hold fast the shortened strands, and it slipped loose. With her free hand, she pulled free the dagger on her belt, turned, and slashed wildly at the presence behind her. The chest of the reaching count opened in a spray and splatter of hot wax in place of blood.

Juliet let loose a resounding wail. But it was powered by more than just fear; rage filled in equal measure.

"You will not have me!" she cried, beating his arms down with the torch. "You will not have me!"

She put the blade in his belly, twisting a hole throughout which more wax did spew.

Showing no sign of pain, Count Paris pressed on, shouting, "Juliet, oh Juliet! My sweet betrothed!"

Wielding torch and dagger, she fended as she backed up, her heels inches from the descending stairs. Paris rushed forth, moaning and leaking and proclaiming his love. Juliet stepped to the side and beat him about the shoulders with her torch, screaming, "You will not have me!"

Paris fell down the steps, his body twisting and breaking and rupturing as it tumbled.

All fear was gone, yet her rage remained. Juliet descended, her torch growing brighter with each step, until it seemed she held a beaming sun in her upraised hand. The torch was more to her than a weapon, more than salvation—it was liberty. She drew closer to the mangled form of Count Paris on the floor, his body melted from the heat of her blazing instrument, until only a face of a man remained, floating in a pool of hot wax.

"Even with my father's blessing, I was never thine," she said, slipping her dagger into its sheath.

She took the torch in both hands, took a deep breath, and snapped that face in twain.

For a brief moment, she stood and wondered why she had been brought back from death whole and healthy, and why Paris returned as a monster. Then she took her leave of House Montague, of Verona, and of this very story.

In the morning, when Lord Romeo and his men returned from a long night of decapitating cats and splitting rats, he first found the cooled and solid pool of wax by the stair. Then, he found his mother's violated and mutilated corpse in her bedroom. Lastly, he found Juliet's letter on their bed, where it did read:

Inquisitor Rosaline,

On the case of the supposedly risen Romeo and Juliet, I have consulted two of my most informed masters on the subject of marriage, Heaven above us, and whether marriage vows continue when passing through the gates of Paradise.

In a lifetime, a man can take several wives should he out-live each in succession. However, because Our Father in heaven doth see polygamy in life or in everlasting eternity as a sin, that a man would <u>not</u> be married to any of his wives once he joins them in God's abode eternal. Therefore, in its unswerving wisdom, the church hath determined that all marriages end at death.

And thus, a speedy matrimonial exchange of vows is strongly encouraged for the young couple, should it be proven that they were indeed dead. Death, of course, has divorced them from their vows made before Friar Lawrence. New vows, particularly in front of proper assembly of families, are expected.

With all due Blessings,

Pope Alexander VIII

By the third time Lord Romeo read the letter, his wits became diseased, his heart was clept in twain, and he no longer knew a hawk from a hand saw. The weight of his madness grew so heavy, that Atlas would not have traded burdens with him.

"Stars!" he shouted as his men restrained him. "All the stars be damned! All the stars be damned!"

Benvolio, his cousin and the last Montague sane and living, in desperation and grief, retrieved the last of Romeo's father's sleeping doses. It took three before the young lord was finally pacified. Hours later, when Romeo awakened, his madness had cooled and was now tempered to a fine edge. Thus he addressed his men:

"I know now why heaven sent me back. 'Twas not to live a long and happy life with wife and family, but to experience the anguish I caus'd them with my selfish suicide. I died, and everyone did suffer. Now, everyone dies around me or disappears to places beyond my knowing, and I suffer. This hath all been the star's design. These stars are Jove's wheels, his spheres of fate. I defied those stars when I first took my life, and I will defy them again. Benvolio, I name thee heir to the fortunes of House Montague and House Capulet. Keep them well and live to great prosperity. I will not need gold where I am going, only my sword."

Still shaken by the deaths of his lord uncle and lady aunt, Benvolio knelt before his cousin and wept upon his knee.

"Oh, misfortunate Romeo! Go not again to that realm beyond life. Live! Live! Kill not the only family I have left. Slay not again thy gracious self!"

Romeo laughed deep and resoundingly, a slight trail of drool pouring from the corner of his well-formed mouth, his piercing eyes twitching with mismatched expressions. "I go not to heaven, hell, or purgatory, coz. I shall endeavor the adventure of reclaiming my lost and fragile Juliet. I will woo her again. And when she hath been retriev'd, I shall keep her and myself far from Verona e'ermore."

His mad smile widened. "But first I will send Rosaline to heaven with a message for the Saint Peter: That neither fates, nor stars, nor God himself should e'er tempt a man as desperate as Romeo of Montague!"

CHAPTER 25

ADVENTS

Throughout the day and all across the cursed city, everyone was preparing for the culmination of their various and conflicting goals, inductions, plots, schemes, and devices.

Through the North gates, the Papal Army filed in a column of tall muscle, gleaming steel, and blond hair nearly stark white in the light of the cold morning sun. In the now empty house of Capulet, they set up their barracks. There, they awaited orders from the Lady Inquisitor.

In her office in the church, Rosaline poured over her various volumes of geometric lore, charters on witch detection, and other ancient secrets both esoteric and arcane. As she did so, she had every nun, friar, priest, and lay priest scurrying throughout the city in search of the ingredients asked for by the Apothecary now in the church's service.

In his laboratory, using eldritch instruments with precise measurements, the fey-possessed Apothecary combined and wielded the four fundamental elements, the ground roots of three mystical trees, twelve powders pulverized from twelve zodiacal stones, and eleven secret herbs and spices to create his supreme substance—a cure above all cures—though it was not the cure promised and commissioned.

Distilled into a great iron cauldron, simmered the secret substance, a singular brew that had not been crafted since before the advent of humanity.

O'er the steaming pot the old man hovered his bent and porous nose. Inhaling deeply, the Apothecary smiled through his unkempt beard.

"My mind doth flood with this aromatic spring, replenishing wither'd memories to new life bring. When nature was timeless and ever young, before words of man were spoke or sung."

Henri, like a curious cat, shuffled in pacing coil about the man and pot. "What doth it do, this brew you stew?"

"The knowing of that is not for you," the master said with a twinkle. "Art thou ready to depart, Henri? Has thou mapp'd out thy route? The water ways beneath this city are dark and extensive."

The great beast wagged its jagged tail. "With these eyes, I am never lost."

The old man smiled warmly. "And you realize that one or both of our destructions might come in this grand execution?"

Henri dropped his long head in thought. "I... remember a simpler time, before my revival. I see in my memory the great river in which I was born, in which I grew, mated, hunted, and, in the end, was hunted by Man. Death was merely the end of pain, but also happiness. Thou hast afforded me vengeance on Man with this charm'd life I am presently enjoying. Man hath wounded beast and sprite. 'Tis natural they should unite against him. And if I die tomorrow, it will be for thee and not in vain."

Wordless, Queen Mab commanded the hand of the old man to pet lovingly the monster's snout. Together, they went to the deepest part of the building, a dark place that stank of mold and waste. With a grunting effort, the Apothecary opened an iron hatch that opened up to the city sewer. Into it and darkness, Henri slithered.

In the comfortable confines of the Montague palazzo, Romeo sat brooding upon the staircase, his disturbed gaze fixed upon the solid pool of wax yet on the stony floor. He knew neither what to think of it nor the wax found upon and within his mother's corpse. Though he knew of similar murders most gruesome and foul, the slightest notion as to the source evaded him.

With caution and concern, his cousin, Benvolio, approached him. "Good cousin, thy face betrays thoughts most painful and heavy. Please, share that burden with me, that we might distribute its contents with reason and wisdom.

"Fie!" Romeo said with a shrugging scoff. "Would that this yoke of mystery be doffed and forgotten. Only Juliet matters now. That and Rosaline's demise."

"Why murder the Inquisitor?"

149

"Because she dared sow doubt in my poor love's heart. She robbed me of my Juliet with guile and obscure law. I'll put my sword through her chaste and cold heart, then flee to freedom."

"But her lictors, her town guards, those might Papal soldiers—how wilt thou escape their retribution?"

Romeo grinned, his face handsome, yet queerly uneven. "I've outrun the law before, coz. The only things swifter than my sword hand are my legs."

Benvolio's eyes lowered to the wax pond. He shuddered. "Juliet's nurse since childhood, Lady Capulet, her mother, and thine own sweet mother, too. All they maternal figures in Juliet's life, all sealed in the same fate. All, I dare say, were at odds with her, out of her favor, when they met their ends.

Romeo regarded his cousin, his stare quickly becoming a glare. "Art thou saying Juliet murder'd them all? That she hath been the one stealing candles and stopping the orifices of various women and ladies throughout Verona?"

Benvolio stepped back, his breath seizing. "Oh! Nay, coz! To no such conclusion was my reason aim'd. I was but trying to find a rhythm or rhyme to these terrible deeds."

Though Benvolio spoke the truth, the jumbled machinery in Romeo's mind cranked and turned to a settled outcome of lunar deduction. His eyes bulged and welled with hot tears. His trembling hands did cover his quivering lips. He let out a hollow cry.

"Oh, Saints be scurg'd and Baptist be drown'd! What if Juliet did commit the murders? She is a Capulet, after all, just like Rosaline and Tybalt! Oh, wisdom oft comes too late for man when his be damn'd by blind love and dreamer's fancy. I admit now… I admit now…" Romeo shut his eyes, forcing the words from his broken brain with great effort. "I admit now that I hardly knew the girl. I still hardly know her! Oh, Benvolio, there is such relief in finding and allowing truth! And more truth I will find when I find Juliet. I will make her talk to get the truth. Then, I will make her scream, either in lover's embrace or by justice of my rapier! Ha!"

Shortly after, good-natured Benvolio went to his room to cry and pray himself to sleep, for never did he feel so alone and helpless.

Below three lit windows of his favorite brothel, Mercutio stood in darkness, smiling. In his worm-infested arms, he cradled three rats who all regarded their master attentively. The cursed ritorno's grin was full of fond memory, boyish triumph, and writhing grubs.

"Here," he said to his pets. "Here did I frequent when my loins and purse were full. Here, did I dull my loneliness. Here, Romeo would have thriv'd in mind and spirit, finding that women are not angels or saints of idol worship, but human beings with the same failings as we men. Had he the nerve to accompany me here, he would have lost his unhealthy appetite for love. We would have stayed happy bachelors by the graces of pretty whores. He would not have married that Capulet, and I would not have been stabbed by one. All would be well still."

He shrugged his shoulder, still smiling. "'Tis a shame I died hating everyone, now I am stuck that way until Queen Mab dismisses me. Ha! 'Tis a shame none believ'd me when I warn'd them of her."

He took a rat by the tail and lifted to his putrid face. "Now, get you to my lady Anna's chamber and nibble her sweet ears. She loved when I did that."

Spinning the rat o'er head, he threw it as David threw his stone up, and it went through the lighted window. He pulled another rat and said, "Up you go, my friend, to the nest of Voila, the most voluptuous song-bird in Verona. Make her sing by gnawing her teats."

He tossed it through the second window.

Holding up the third and final rat, he commanded "Now, to you I say, chew the toes of Miranda, for although comely, I always thought her feet too big. Shorten them."

Once the third rat was upward tossed, Mercutio turned and departed the scene as shrieks and screams broke from yonder windows. His laughter was hidden by the frenzied wailing.

And high above Verona's streets, on a window sill long and wide, Tybalt the Dark Prince of Cats lay on his side, one of his long legs extended straight up toward heaven, his codpiece damp from his continuous licking.

CHAPTER 26

THE INQUISITION OF VERONA

The morning stirred sweet, soft breezes, and not a cloud dared dally before the beaming sun. It was a weather that permitted anything and everything to occur. Of what would happen, the people of the city were forewarned. Yet when the thunderous knocks of halberds and staves shook their doors, all were cowed and frightened.

The Papal Army had little resistance drawing forth the wretched remnants of families from their homes. Nearly all people were too weak or sick to resist. Those few who did resist, or ventured escape, were cloven through head and trunk and left to bleed where they lay. The orders and actions of the Swiss soldiers came with perfect precision and timing, with a rhythm more mechanical than musical, as if they were powered by gears instead of faith and blood. Their assortment of blades seemed both impressive in utility and abundant in variety. Indeed, this Swiss army was a knife fitted with many blades, each with a purpose.

As the Papal guards drove their flocks toward the city's heart, a Spaniard by name of Fernando De Soto stopped walking. In his life and home country, Fernando had seen and lived through too many an inquisition. He demanded to leave the city, expressing no desire to take part in what was to come. He tried bribery, but the Swiss guards, unmoved, commanded him to resume the forced march to the city square. When he drew his rapier, he soon found that all his refined mastery of Spanish fencing meant little to a Swiss pikeman. The great spear punched many times in rapid flurry through the Spaniard's body as though it were cheese, leaving many holes before Fernando's legs gave out in death.

The crowd to be tested and cleansed of bodily and spiritual impurities consisted of less than a thousand wretched men and women—all children and the very old having already succumb to the plague. They were weary yet wary, miserable yet hopeful, faithful yet terrified. For they were told that if they were to survive the inquisition planned, they would surely be saved.

When all were assembled on the open stone floor that was the town square and Verona's Heart, the people beheld a tall cross of iron easily two men high. By it was a massive arcane circle, a complex geometric design composed of all the salt gathered from every home in Verona. The circle expanded to a diameter of twenty feet. By that was the great stone fountain alive with arching jets of water. Around it stood several priests, casting blessings into the water like wishing coins.

Rosaline stood in her usual attire, a modest black dress with matching veil, a golden crucifix and a ring as her only adornments. Behind her were her three lictors. Behind them were twenty armed guards, half Swiss mercenaries, the other half, sons of Verona. At her left stood Friar John, looking disconcerted and anxious. At her right stood the Apothecary stirring his cauldron of remedy with a long pewter ladle.

Spreading her arms and stepping forward, the Inquisitor of Verona drew a hush from the afflicted congregation.

"My children," the lady began. "This test of faith and faithfulness shall be a simple one. Behold the iron cross standing erect and strong. Behold the circle of salt, laid out in patterns both holy and mathematically relevant. Behold our fountain roiling with water cold and pure. Iron, salt, and water: the components of blood—the blood of our savior, Jesus Christ. Pass through the blood of our lord, and thou shalt be cleansed and saved by this goodly Apothecary's blessed elixir."

"All will be called to this test. All must approach when called. Refuse, and you will be slain outright. Kiss the iron cross without it burning thy lips. If its property doth burn thee, then thou art surely bewitched or a witch thyself. Walk into the salt circle and out again. If you can do this, then the second part of the test is passed. If you can do one, the other, or neither, then surely a devil is in thee, and it will be cut loose with a mortal blow. Finally, thou all must dunk thy heads in the waters of this fountain made holy today. If it doth not boil the flesh from thy skulls, then surely thou art devout and obedient servants of the Lord and His church. Step then forward and receive thy cure from this Apothecary's ladle. Fail this test in any way, and thou art surely Mab's minion. And death will fall upon thee swift and true!"

The Apothecary felt the countless eyes of the crowd upon him, yet he bothered not to look up from his stirring. He could feel their desire for what he brewed, their thirst for a cure to their ills. Placidly, he grinned.

One at a time, the people were called; the entire remainder of the crowd watching as they kissed the cross, passed through the salt circle, dunked their heads, and received the Apothecary's cure. It was not until each took their dose from his ladle that the next person called.

An hour did pass, and after most of the people had been thus tested and processed, none had burnt their lips on the iron, none had become trapped in the circle, and none were ill-affected by the blessed water save for its seasonal chill. Indeed, the only part of the course that seemed effectual was the distributing and partaking of the Apothecary's cure. For when the sick and afflicted did imbibe the dram, within minutes they felt the seeping relief of remedy. All ill symptoms disappeared.

As the test was passed again and again, the Lady Inquisitor looked none too pleased. With each passing person, the next met the diving challenge with less fear, until at last, only two men remained.

Benvolio and his lord cousin stood in stern silence as a dozen Swiss pikes drew near them. From afar, Romeo saw the glare emanating from Rosaline's cold dark eyes.

"Let the *ritorno* come forth!" the Inquisitor commanded, her teeth bared in judicial hunger. "Let it be known if his resurrection was divine or a work of witchcraft!"

"This was all plann'd for me—was it not, Rosaline Capulet?" Romeo shouted the words in hateful defiance. The pikes of Papal soldiers stopped mere inches from his being, yet he acknowledged them not.

"Oh, let me go first, I beseech you!" Benvolio called, placing a hand on Romeo's shoulder. "For if Romeo be accurs'd, then I, too, am accurs'd. His blood his mine. His misfortunes and his woes and his joys art mine, as well."

The Inquisitor scoffed before nodding in acquiescence. "Blessed are the peace keepers. Come, good Benvolio, and thy quality shall be prov'd."

The pike parted, and Benvolio hugged his lord cousin. "We've nothing to fear, coz," he said. "I shall embrace thee again in a minute's time."

Displaying courage serene and noble, the humble Benvolio advanced to the great cross of iron. Calmly and hesitating not, he placed a lingering, chaste kiss on the chilled metal beam. His full, youthful lips burnt not, but stayed as smooth and undamaged as an infant's skin. He then walked across the entire breadth of the strange geometric circle, showing no sign of hindrance walking in or out. Finally, doffing his hat and steeling himself for the cold rush of water, he approached the grand fountain that was the crown of the town square. With reverence to the now holy waters that bubbled and splashed about, he placed both hands on the fountain's stony rim and bowed deeply and humbly in saintly submission to the order of his god's holy church.

159

Just before his wavy hair touched the ever-shifting surface of the water, something shot out from it and took hold of his head. Benvolio felt as if an iron vice fitted with spikes had latched onto his skull and, fast as lightning, that vice rolled with a thousand pounds of sinuous muscle, turning the Montague's head around and tearing it halfway off the body. A great splash erupted from the fountain as the lifeless corpse dropped before it, and out of the blasting wave leapt the long and scaly form of Henri, the Alligator. Voices raised in wondrous horror as the great beast landed upon the street-stones, crushing a priest beneath his bulk.

The crowd wailed in terror, the soldiers trembled and gripped fast their arms. Rosaline bared her teeth in outrage through her own fear, and Romeo screamed in shocked agony and maddening anguish.

"Benvolio!" the last Montague cried. He drew his sword, forgetting the numerous pikes about his person. The pikemen who held them were too distracted by the monster to notice.

"Humans of Verona!" the giant reptile proclaimed. "Thy crimes against nature and the realms of beast and fey ye shall answer for this hour! By high order of Queen Mab, I deliver unto thee cold-blooded vengeance!"

With an appalling undulation of his long frame, Henri opened his lethal mouth and vomited two piles of bones upon the ground.

A Swiss guard wielding a partisan charged the great alligator's side. With blinding speed, Henri batted the weapon aside with his tail, bit deep into the soldier's thigh, and then rolled his great body upon the stones, crushing and mangling the man.

More cries pierced the heavens as the two slime-covered piles of bones pieced together, animating into a pair of walking skeletons. One of them held a dagger, which unexpectedly burst into flame.

Frightened, the crowd turned from the abominable scene, trying to run through the streets and back to their homes. But every stone of the square was covered with the hissing shapes of countless rats and cats. Even the buildings surrounding them spewed the malevolent pests from their doors and windows.

"Stand thy ground!" Rosaline shouted, drawing her dagger and raising it aloft. "Stand thy ground!" She cried again, and the soldiers, both local and papal, heard her words and felt the bravery in them.

She called the names of her lictors, each man drawing his foil in turn. She pointed to the great monster by the fountain. Her nerves were steel. Her eyes and voice blazed with authority. "Arpeggio!" she said, and the three lictors charged Henri, no sign of fear on their faces. As Rosaline watched on, the Apothecary stood behind her, his wispy beard hiding a thin smile.

CHAPTER 27

THE ENDLESS SONG

Romeo's mind was a whirling stew of grief, rage, and horror. The once stalwart and grave Swiss guards standing about him fought in vain against the onslaught of rats chewing at their heels and cats mauling their groins and loins, their great pikes useless against the scurrying terrors. Romeo had no such trouble, for his rapier was nimble and quick, as he had been hunting these creatures for the past week. Despite his inner ruin, Romeo's talent with fencing did not falter. Every rat or cat that drew near him was immediately beheaded, impaled, or split in twain.

One of the slimy skeletons the alligator had vomited approached him. Though eyeless and lipless, Romeo swore that he recognized the horrific thing. As it stepped closer, the underlying swarm of vermin dispersed between them.

"Benvolio is dead! There, art thou happy?" the skull said incredulously.

Romeo's eyebrows raised. "That voice…"

"Thy mother is dead! There, art thou happy?"

"Oh, no," Romeo whimpered. The smell of decay filled the air, causing the young lord's gorge to rise.

"Thy father is dead! There, art thou happy?"

"Oh, ghostly friar! Lifelong friend and my father-in-spirit! Friar Lawrence!"

The skeleton placed its hands together, as if in prayer. "Thy Juliet has fled thee. Thy marriage and love is undone. She goes now a free spirit with Mab's blessing. She will know many adventures and many lovers. Thou hast lost her forever. There, art thou happy?"

"You lie!" Romeo cried, all his grief and terror turning into rage. Swinging wildly, he beat the boney form apart, scattering the parts this way and that. As he did so, his shouts of rage turned into wails of sobbing. He fell to his knees, broken in mind and spirit.

The knife-brandishing skeleton of Valentine was more passive in speech, less so in action. He ran with grace and speed to rival Atalanta during her fabled hunts, and just as deadly was his predatory skill. With such ease did he avoid the numerous polearms and swords born by the men-at-arms that the act of assassinating them looked more dance than skirmish. One by one, the soldiers dropped, their hearts split open like ripe peaches on a summer night. Yet, not a drop of juice was spilt, for the dagger billowed ever a cloud of black smoke and sealed each wound with cautery withdrawal.

Rosaline watched as her lictors encircled the hissing beast. "Skewer it as St. George pierc'd the dragon!" she urged.

Henri paced in a wary circle as the three bodyguards surrounded him. His glass eyes blazed with awful light as he divined where each one stood in relation

164

to him. The first lictor darted in from behind. With a lash of his tail, Henri tripped the man into falling. The second man advanced sideways. With his front most teeth, Henri caught the man by the elbow, but not before the foil's tip pierced his belly. With a wrenching jerk, the alligator tore the arm from its socket. As this happened, the third lictor's sword penetrated the monster's other side. As Henri answered the assault by disemboweling the assailant with a bloody bite to the abdomen, the lictor who was tripped rose to his feet to deliver a downward stab to the beast's spine. As the two other lictors fell to succumb to their mortal wounds, the third let go of his blade, seeing now that the arpeggio was complete. Yet, even with three swords in him, Henri did not slow, and like a whirling dervish from hell's first circle, he turned to pounce upon and devour the last lictor. As the terrified bodyguard was swallowed whole, he found the three sharp points of the embedded foils waiting to greet him within the cramped confines of the monster's stomach.

Rosaline's perfectly poised shoulders, for the first time ever, drooped in shocked disappointment. "Shit," she uttered.

She heard a scream beside her and beheld Friar John wresting a mauling cat from his throat. The holy man pulled off the feline with the ease granted by panic-fed strength, but not without incidentally aiding the creature in severing his main cables. The friar fell backward, bleeding, gurgling, and dying.

All around, the crowd was gathered in a mass of huddled panic as cats and rats swarmed over the flailing bodies of soldiers both local and Papal. The vile pests were keeping the citizens in check and slaying her army like swarms of locusts devour millet.

Behind her, a voice started singing. When she turned, she found that voice did not match the face. For the voice was of a young woman, and the face was of a crazed elderly man.

Swinging his spotted hands in a whimsical fashion, he sang with a volume and power beyond his mortal frame.

"Endless song, Endless song,

'Tis my right to do you wrong,

Endless song, Endless song,

Sing it loud and sing it long,

Those who drank in huddled throng,

Hear this song, sing this song,

Sing it loud and sing it long!"

Half the screaming in the square ceased with chilling abruptness. The amassed remainder of Verona's citizens stood in still silence, their expressions queer. Then, as a chorus of solemn monks, they joined their voices together with the eerie hymn.

"Endless song, endless song,

'Tis our right to do you wrong,

Endless song, endless song,

Sing it loud and sing it long,

We who drank in huddled throng,

Hear this song, sing this song,

Sing it loud and sing it long!"

To Rosaline, the tune was a wild and formless working of sound and ether trapped within the confines of rhythm, melody, and words. More lay beyond what her cold and calculating mild could perceive in that choral structure. That structure was all her senses could detect and understand. Yet, there was some part of her, a part like an underdeveloped muscle that sensed a transmogrification in the balance of what she perceived as nature.

She turned to the Apothecary, their faces mere paces apart as the Endless Song swelled about them. "What are you doing to them?" she asked.

The Apothecary grinned, scooped up a measure of his remedy broth with his ladle and responded with a voice of polluted honey and corroded bells.

"Have a drink and ye will see,

Have a drink – a drink on me,

Be not enslaved – instead fly free,

Oh, have a drink and free ye'll be!"

Glancing up and down between the offered brew and the eerie face of the old man, the Inquisitor gasped and held forth her dagger. "Mab!" she cried.

Bleary-eyed and cackling, the elderly form gave her answer. "In bed asleep we dream things true!" As David had slung his stone, so did the alchemist fling the serving of the eldritch stew, sending it in splattering ruination on Rosaline's modest black gown. She seized in insult and revulsion, backing a pace as she did so.

She felt her feet crush something beneath her. She looked down to see the rocky grains of salt piled inches high in curved rows. "The circle!" she thought, and backed deeper into the confines of that complex geometrical mandala of protection. Once in the salt seal's center, a renewed calm bestilled her startled nerves despite the horrors surrounding her. "Here I am safe, but what of my fair Verona?"

The soldiers were fallen, now reduced to not more than settled heaps swarmed by chewing rats and suckling cats. Swords, pikes, halberds and partisans lay as still as their wielders. All screams of battle and pain were over.

The common people of Verona, the remaining sons and daughters of that once fair city, stood in entranced choral mass. The Endless Song continued, as endless songs are want to do.

Endless Song, Endless Song,

Sing it loud and sing it long,

Endless song, Endless Song,

'Tis our right to do you wrong!

All their faces were blue of pallor with entranced eyes bulging. Higher and faster they sang. 'Twas when the lot of them did change to visages of purple did Rosaline realize "They doth breath out to sing, yet they do not breathe in! They sing themselves to death, expending every breath!"

With horror and outrage, the fair maid of the cloth did watch and listen as the Endless Song robbed the remainder of her people of life-breath. One by one, they collapsed, still mouthing the words as the light faded from their vacant stares. When the last of them fell in croaking death, the song continued in eerie silence. Then like pops of gas in a crackling fire, the eyeballs of the entranced dead burst in wet ejaculations of blood and tears. And out from the bleeding sockets flew thousands of little winged things that took up the Endless Song with their queer and merry voices. Rising high into the air like clusters of ember, the swarm of flying things laughed and sang and chittered in tongues unheard for untold centuries.

"Fairies!" Rosaline exclaimed in gasping whisper.

Hopping and dancing just outside the salt circle, the Apothecary laughed in the voice of his possessor.

Alive again my ancient kin,

169

Born from mortal coils undone,

Wisely judg'd my ancient grudge,

Now the cunning war is won!

A way off, kneeling, Romeo felt a tap of steel on his slumped shoulder.

Romeo looked up to see Tybalt Capulet, cat-faced with fangs bloody and eyes burning like coals of a smith. The unholy ritorno held a rapier not inches from Romeo's face.

Expressionless and with cheeks wet with tears, Romeo shook his head. "So, 'tis true that thou didst escape the grave, too, eh, Tybalt? Was it God or the devil who render'd us back? Or was it yon swarm of caroling fey who magicked our rising from death's eternal crypts?"

There was dire silence betwixt them before an unseen sword point poked the Montague's buttock.

Romeo leapt to his feet, hopping and screaming from the startling sting. He turned to see worm-infested Mercutio grinning at him, his drawn sword tipped with wet red.

"Mercutio!" Romeo cried, and his tears started anew. "Oh, Mercutio, dearest of friends! My only joy left in this world! Why? Why has this happened to Verona? Why all this death and magic and misery?"

The maggoty face shifted from one of comic glee to one of dire import. "This, my love-struck lack-wit, is the culmination of centuries of schemes through dreams. This, quite simply, is the work of Queen Mab, whose mischief hath plagued the brains of Verona's citizens since mankind first did settle here. Our long ago forbearers brought vengeance manifest."

Romeo shook the tears from his fair face. "But why save me for last? Why was I forc'd to watch all my love torn from my restor'd heart? Is this hell? Is this my punishment for murder and suicide?"

An eyebrow of Mercutio arched. "Nay, wretch'd one. Remember when I did warn thee of her? When I tried with all my passion to convey to thee? Dost thou remember my forbearance of the fairy Queen Mab?"

"Aye!" Romeo answered, weeping from the strain of his present situation. "I remember, Mercutio. Every word thou didst e'er speak to me is etched upon my broken heart!"

Mercutio's milk-white eyes widened. "Remember what thou didst dare call her?"

Romeo opened his mouth to speak, but his friend threw the answer out.

"You called her NOTHING! I talked of Queen Mab, and thou didst say that I talk'd of NOTHING! Thou durst not call the queen of all fairies NOTHING. To do so, to disbelieve so, is the cheiftest of ignorances. 'Twas that same disbelief that so long ago diminish'd her kind. Those with sense of mind at least entertain their possibility. But you, oh fool! You have attracted her attention and earned her wrath because thou seest only with thine eyes. Thou dost love only with thine eyes. Thou knowest only with thine eyes!"

A growl of impatience came from Tybalt, to which Mercutio nodded and said, "Romeo, thy end is at hand. You stand once more between me and Tybalt. He and I will cross swords once more. We will stab and flay each other's flesh until we are but bones fencing eternally throughout the ruins of Verona. But first, we must swat the fly who interrupted us."

Before Lord Romeo of Montague could protest by words or his sword, the cold blades of Tybalt and Mercutio ran him through. Just as swift, they removed their weapons from his burdensome torso and let him fall dying upon the cold street.

As life departed and death entered, Romeo smiled with happy, mad eyes and said, "Oh, sweet oblivion! Thou art fairer than Juliet e'er was! Her brightness did but blind me, for now I see that seeing is for fools. Take me under thy black wing, and let me be blind as the stones beneath."

Thus perished Romeo of Montague.

Locking their horrific eyes, Tybalt and Mercutio inched toward one another, their swords presented, both smiling.

"Wait!" shouted the Apothecary. "There is yet one more enemy untouch'd by our spell. Come ye all, my monsters and minions, so that this pretty and chaste woman of the church may know how true power feels!"

Rosaline stood firm in her complex circle of salt as the Apothecary, Tybalt, Mercutio, Valentine, and Henri took places about the grand design. Above her, the clouding swarm of newborn fairies sang and laughed down at her with pinched evil faces. With dagger still in hand, she pointed to them all in turn.

She saw that the bones of her army were picked clean, and the rats and cats moved onto the eyeless corpses of the civilian throng.

At this sight, Rosaline sighed as if losing a game of chess. "And the minions of hell did rule the earth for a thousand years."

She looked at the Apothecary, her eyes beaming with pride in the face of defeat. "Thy devilish means bring but temporary glory, Mab. You may slay and command their bodies, but not their souls. That immortal part belongs to God in heaven. Thy gains are not lasting, not eternal."

Mab laughed out through the old man's mouth. "Do you truly believe He loves thee? Protects thee? Do you truly believe you are in accord with His plan? Do you think He even has a plan?"

Rosaline sneered. "I know more than most my age, most my sex. I have studied the slow dances of the stars, the mathematical mysteries of circles and triangles. I am versed in the cosmic spheres and astrological charts. I have memorized all scriptures of my Lord, both canon and apocryphal. And—" she said waving about her dagger. "I have read the tales of all witches and fairies that haunt Europe! This salt circle and my God protect me from you and your foul brood, Mab. You will not kill me this day. There will be justice in thy short future!"

Crossing his spindly arms, the fey-possessed Apothecary stepped forth and over the arcane barrier as though it were dung in the street. "Rosaline, Rosaline. Believe not always what you read—this goes in equal measure to fairy tales and religion. For in truth, they are one in the same, beyond any mortal's understanding. They are dreams, things that control you and things that I control."

As one, the fairy queen's minions entered the circle. With her, they enclosed upon the stunned Inquisitor as fingers close upon a coin.

For Rosaline, it was too much. Tybalt, now cat-faced and vampiric, had once been her brother. Mercutio was a festering mass of worms and putrefied flesh. Valentine was a skeleton dripping with bile. The alligator's glass eyes blazed with eldritch light. The Apothecary's face displayed smug triumph. With her pride and faith broken, a scorn unfathomable compelled her to fight. There was no room for fear, only the contempt of a woman proven wrong by another woman.

With all her hate, she stabbed the old man in the belly. An all-too-human groan escaped his lips, and he collapsed to the ground before her. The others about her stopped yet were in close enough proximity to prevent her escape.

They all watched the old man grow still as he lay upon the ground on his side. Blood escaped about the dagger's hilt. Out from his large and fuzz-adorned ear climbed a shape no larger than an agate stone on the forefinger of an alderman. Covered in orange wax and looking of ill temper, the tiny Queen Mab looked up at the distorted faces high above her.

"Seize her!" she ordered her monsters, and the deed was done. The men grabbed Rosaline's arms and shoulders. Henri seized her leg with his great trap of a mouth just hard enough to hold her fast.

Rosaline screamed. Her pride and authority were lost and forgotten, her anger spent in stabbing the Apothecary of Mantua. All that was left was terror and her voice to express it.

"Peace!" Queen Mab commanded, her voice resounding beyond her size. "The choice is thine, Rosaline!"

Rosaline quieted, her dark eyes betraying helplessness, her lips quivering like a child's.

Mab spoke. "Choose the form of thy death. Shalt Tybalt drain thee of blood from thy white neck? Shalt Mercutio infect thy tender flesh with hungry worms? Shalt Valentine stab thy cruel and cold heart? Or shalt Henri swallow you whole?" The tiny fey cackled and added, "'Tis a shame that Paris perished. Juliet's magic was stronger than his. He would have enjoyed scalding thy virgin insides!"

Her laugh grew like a blazing flame beyond her control, so sweet was her malice and sense of triumph. She gazed into the terrified maid's eyes, basking in her despair like rays of sunshine.

Fast as Mercury's heel, the Apothecary's hand came down upon his cheek as if swatting some vile insect. In the sudden and unexpected blow, Queen Mab was squished against his cheek bone and smeared in gory pieces on to his nose and into his whiskers. His sad and weary eyes looked up at the face of the awe-struck woman and the horrors that held her.

"The world…was not my friend," he said weakly. "Yet…I tried to be a friend to the world, to make it better."

Rosaline's heart swelled. "You did!" she said, her cold countenance shedding tears for the first time in years. "You did, good Apothecary! You slew Queen Mab! Now, her terrors can proceed no more. Go now to Saint Peter's gate, and know that thou art forgiven!"

A tired smile appeared on the old man's face, and there it stayed fixed, even as he died.

Weeping and laughing with relieved joy, Rosaline looked about at the monsters holding her. "She's dead! Dead! She is thy mistress no longer! Now, all of you wretched accursed can return to thy graves, for a slave be not a slave if the master be dead. Rest, you all. Rest in peace eternal."

Smiling sweetly, Mercutio wiped away the tears from her fair cheeks. Speaking loudly and bold, he said, "To rest, to sleep. To sleep, perchance to dream! Aye me, I've a better plan—let's feed her to the alligator, boys!"

The monsters roared in gay approval, Rosaline in shrieking protest. Henri's mouth opened wide as they stuffed her in head first. As the great beast swallowed the struggling meal, Mercutio sang:

Though she be a maid-she doth kick like a slattern,

Her pretty legs swing and stomp air without pattern,

Her heels turn like wheels as if in heat'd passion,

So passes Rosaline in lewd wriggling fashion!

Henri's jaws closed as the twitching feet disappeared down his throat. All laughed at Mercutio's jest. Even Tybalt could not help but titter.

All about them, the plaguing rats and vampiric cats dispersed from the city in a storm of hisses and squeaks that would soon be heard throughout Italia. Mercutio, Valentine, and Tybalt commenced to stab and whittle away at each other's unholy forms until only their cursed spirits remained to haunt Verona ever after. As for Henri, he eventually swam all the way back to Egypt to finally find repose beneath the land's pagan sun.

And high above the defiled corpse of Verona, the fairies scattered to the four winds, still singing their endless song.

Endless Tune, Endless Tune,

Over Earth and Under Moon,

Mendless Wound, Mendless Wound,

We live again to sing and swoon!

Endless Jest, Endless Jest,

Freedom beats beneath our breast,

Endless Jest, Endless Jest,

In Peace a fairy cannot Rest!

Endless Dance, Endless Dance,

Love is but a game of chance,

Endless Dance, Endless Dance,

Roll the dice and bet thy pants!

THE END

About the Author

Aaron Hollingsworth lives in Kansas City, Missouri with his wife and cover artist, Stephanie, and their two sons. Since his youth, the works of The Bard of Avon have continuously inspired him. He acquired permission to write this sequel from William Shakespeare via Ouija board by black candle light. He invites his readers to check out his Facebook fan pages, **Four Winds – One Storm** and **Aaron Hollingsworth – Science Fantasy Writer**.

Made in the USA
Columbia, SC
10 September 2019